Running to Never

Larinna Chandler

YellowFeather Press LLC

This book is dedicated to my soulmate, my true love...my husband Curtis. You're always in my corner, even when I don't think you are. To my beautiful babies; Matthew Ian, Gabriel Skye, Asuka Lynn: You kids are our whole world.

And always, to the memory of our dear friends Cory and Tyler Renard, you will always be missed by your crew, and never forgotten.

"Everything is good Forever"
-Tyler Renard

"That's the thing about the day before your life changes. It feels like any other day"
-Cory Renard

The Holocaust had millions of victims. Most are what we have come to know; Innocent Jewish families, gypsies, the handicapped, and simply those humans who didn't fit the "perfect" German ideal.

There were however many other victims, not as well known. Many German families and soldiers were brought into it, simply because of their own race. They may not have believed in it, but to speak out was a death sentence for their own families. Some helped. Some saved as many as they could, and some good men, as we know, did nothing.

Some men like Josef made sure that the prisoners in their camps had food and water. A few like Kurt Gerstein, an SS officer risked his life time and time again to tell the truth. To make people aware of what was happening. What was truly happening under this terrifying regime. Many simply dismissed his claims. After the war was over Kurt died in a French prison, a war criminal, after spending years trying to prevent the holocaust. It was rumored both that he died of natural causes and also that he was killed by his fellow countrymen for being a traitor. No one will ever know how Kurt died in that prison.

The author Gitta Sereny later wrote:
"Gerstein's life is perhaps the most significant testimonial to the presence of moral convictions and heroism in the midst of the Nazi monstrosities ... a man in Germany who at almost unimaginable personal risk had tried, actively and from the start, to stop Hitler's genocide."

Another man, with an "infamous" name was Albert Goering. He was the younger brother of Hermann Goering. Hermann was the second in command answering to none other than Adolf Hitler himself. Albert used his infamous name, his clout to save people when he could.

These men did exist. Some of them giving even the smallest kindness with no recognition, nor want of any recognition.

The depths of human despair and those evil enough to even fathom it, much less actually go out and do it will hopefully never again happen. Questions will always remain about this bleak time in world history, most questions will remain unanswered. Hanna and Eva could have been anyone. Their story of survival is chronicled over and over again.

Josef and Klaus too, could have existed, and probably did. Men like Gerhard Kurzbach, who were officers and rounded up Jews, not to kill them, but to save them. Men like Karl Plagge who demanded that "workers" in his camp not be mistreated. There were countless others who did such small favors and some incredibly heroic acts to save Jewish prisoners. Such men may have existed; torn not only by duty and honor… but also with common decency and dare I say sense.

Many men, their stories you will never hear. They were found out to be "jew-lovers" and quickly killed by their own party. Killed for believing that no man should be murdered simply because of what he was.

Showing even simple human compassion and empathy was severely and sometimes fatally punished. Those few brave men are who Josef and even Klaus in his cranky old way was modeled after. Good men who were also lost and mostly forgotten in that horrible war.

Any resemblance to any person alive or dead, in this book is purely coincidental. All characters are a work of fiction.

March, 1944 Majdanek Concentration Camp, Poland

The child stirred beside her, snuggling in closer for whatever warmth she could still provide from her own thin body. She wrapped her arms around her only child and fought back tears. Her daughter needed every second of precious rest and she didn't want to wake her up with her sobs.

Hanna had plenty to cry about, these last six months and that horrible lump in her throat never went away.

Her child shifted uncomfortably again under the old threadbare blanket. She sat up on one elbow and carefully pulled the blanket off herself and tucked it around her shivering Eva and then pulled her close to curl around her child once more.

The torn, thin blanket never kept them very warm but she appreciated what warmth it did provide, now that her entire backside was exposed. Only the thin striped uniform covered her, and then just barely.

She fought the lump again, her head lying on her arm right behind her daughter. This was never supposed to be this way. Hanna curled her daughter tighter in her arms and tried to fall back into the fitful sleep she had awoken from.

Morning would come sooner than wanted. It would come even though she didn't want it to arrive at all. How easily she could slip off into a deep sleep and never awaken.

She couldn't do that though. Not to her baby. Eva deserved so much more than she currently had. She didn't need to wake up cold and alone…or worse, wake to find her mother beside her, cold and never to smile down at her again.

The tears she tried to keep in check began to roll over the bridge of her nose and fall onto her cheek. Hanna knew of many other mothers who had gone that way.

There were also those who had carefully covered their sleeping children's faces until the cruelty of this existence was no more for their unfortunate souls.

Hanna couldn't do that. It wasn't that she hadn't thought of it; but she simply couldn't do it. Eva was her whole world, but was she being selfish keeping her here?

She had to keep hoping. She had to keep living. She could not give up. She could not lose that small shred of hope, no matter how fragile it was. Besides her beautiful and solemn little Eva, it was the only thing she had left. Hope.

Some of the other women in "camp" clicked their tongues at her, scolding without any words needing to be said. Reminding her that her faith and hope were wasted; there was no rescue coming. There never would be, and she was a fool for thinking otherwise.

That small shred of hope was all she had though. All she had left. Of course, it would be a cold day in hell before and even if any hope of rescue would ever be realized. But what did she have to lose holding that hope in her heart? She was already in hell, and it was spelled Majdanek. It was run by monsters. Monsters disguised as humans.

Chapter 1

"Josef stoppen!" Klaus ran to his friend, entreating him to stop and talk. "He wants you to go to him now!"

"Nein! That piss ant has nothing I want to hear!" Josef continued to his Steyr.

"They're sending us to Majdanek. You were promoted to General. You outrank the piss ant now. You are sure you want to storm off and not talk to him?" Klaus laughed as he ground his cigarette butt into the soot and dirt covered snow by the outskirts of camp. "You have to go to the Commander though now; he's requested you report and get your travel orders."

"What?" Josef stopped with his foot half way into his Steyr and turned to look at his friend. "I'm a General now, you low ranking hund?"

"Call me dog one more time you horse's ass!" Klaus laughed and ran his hands over his shaved head. "I still don't know why you get to keep your hair!"

"Well, I'm not lying in every random harlots bed like you are, collecting lice, hund!"

Klaus punched his friend in the shoulder. They had been friends for as long as they remembered. When he was sent to the battle front to keep the Allied pigs from overtaking their country, Josef went with him. He knew Josef's heart as well as he did his own. Josef was the only brother he had ever had, brothers by loyalty though not by blood. He was quick to defend the defenseless, just as Klaus was quick to look away when Josef would cover a hovering Jewish child back up, pretending he did not see.

Klaus didn't like Josef's interest in the lesser people, seeing it as a threat at times to his own standing under Hitler's third Reich. One didn't simply challenge the ruling, it was obvious after all that a cleansing should happen and was happening, then the United States and everyone else poked their damn noses in and were sending men and boys to fight and kill his own men!

It was the only thing they had ever argued about, Josef and his bleeding heart, trying to save the world one 'Untermensch' or subhuman at a time. Klaus turned and walked back to the barracks with his friend. He might hate Josef's stance, but he was his friend. His brother and his brother in arms; he would remain loyal; good friends were hard to find. Josef just needed some more sense talked into him over time. After he joined with Klaus, he went through the ranks just as quickly, sometimes even pulling Klaus along with him. He was an excellent soldier, with the exception of his poor judgment where the Jews were concerned.

Josef rubbed his nose as he walked next to his friend. He knew Klaus and he knew the sideways glances, harshly- yet silently, chiding him for his softness. Klaus was his friend, in some way he always would be...but deep down they both knew that sooner or later their loyalty to both each other and their country would be at odds.

Rather than bring anything up, Josef just walked quietly along, his hair slapping rhythm high on his temples as he walked. What had begun as a way of infuriating his superior officer began to define him. He was not a man to be trifled with. He would fight and it didn't matter who with. Many of men had sported trophies of his anger on their faces. After these last years, no one even bothered him about his hair, and he never bothered to shave it again, just trimming it now and then when he felt like it.

To remain, just barely within the standard codes. It was perhaps one of the only things the men agreed on. They were their own men and had a tendency to interpret the rules how they saw fit. Other men either respected them or didn't. There was not much black and white with Josef and Klaus. They and their actions were all but a gray area.

Some of the fights he *had* initiated and was known to be quick tempered and a devil in a fight, no one but Klaus realized those officers who had felt the wrath of Josef's fists had all 'earned' it in Josef's mind. Josef hated the War. Hated the treatment of the Jews, but at least by going through the army regime and working his way up he had been able to save lives.

Klaus knew, and Klaus hated it. They had an unspoken bond, neither one of them spoke to each other about the crimes they had committed. Klaus would cover Josef's back by a quick distraction so Josef wouldn't be seen assisting a Jew and Josef had made sure Klaus went up in rank right along with him. He was the best of the best. He had wanted to be in the army since a young child and Josef facilitated that for him. Klaus kept Josef's dangerous secrets, although sometimes grudgingly.

They stopped at the wooden plank door, and smiled at each other. They were off on another adventure. War was not an adventure of course, but sitting around cooling their heels for the six months in this stinking regiment was getting damn old.

Josef stopped to adjust his uniform and tuck his hair under his hat. He flicked his cuffs, adjusted his lapels and knocked briskly at the door. Klaus leaned on the opposite wall and lit up another cigarette. He inhaled deeply and watched his brother enter the office.

"Come in, sit down" The old commander gestured towards the worn chair opposite his own mahogany desk. "I've read over your files and I must admit I am impressed. I've also seen a few mentions of some other activities you may have indulged in a time or two."

The commanding officers eyes drilled into Josef's own. Josef fought the urge to squirm or look away but did neither. He flatly returned the stare and said not a word. He would let the commanding officer look away first. The commander held his gaze for a second and stared back down on to the files in his hands. Josef watched the commander pace back and forth a time or two in front of his mahogany desk. He stopped, twisted a tendril of his grey mustache and looked at Josef again.

"There's a great many notes that are in here but your commanders have chosen to ignore them for whatever reason. You are well aware that some of your clandestine activities are treasonous. In fact, some of your other officers have scribbled a few notes. This puts me in a bit of a quandary."

Once more the commander looked at Josef, but this time looked him up and down. "I see a worthy soldier; a soldier I'd be proud to promote to General." The old commander cleared his throat and walked back around his desk to sit on his old wooden chair that seemed as out of place as the grizzled old man did behind the shiny desk.

Josef watched; his blue grey eyes shaded by the brim of his officer's hat as the old man began to fill a pipe. The commander lit the pipe and inhaled deeply.

"See, what we have is a problem. Your other commanding officers liked you, and even looked the other way. I'm not sure they should have." The old commander paused, sat back on his chair and inhaled deeply again.

"Ich weiß nicht was Sie meinen, Sir" Josef calmly spoke.

"You don't know what I mean! I know very damn well you know exactly what I mean! You've been helping the Jewish pigs!" The commanders shouted. "I'm going to have you hanged for treason, officer or not!"

Josef had known the price he would pay would come due one day. Still he sat quietly. To jump to defend himself would just anger the commander further and speed up his own death sentence.

Suddenly the commander rose out of his chair, surprisingly agile for his age and pompous belly. He walked to the door and thrust it open. "Guard!" he yelled to Klaus! "Get in here", you are to take this man to Lublin and he will be hanged for his crimes!"

Klaus warily entered the room, searching Josef's face, hoping to find some kind of answer there or at least how he should respond.

"Soldier!" the old commander barked! "At attention!" Klaus quickly raised his hand in a smart salute. "At ease!"

The old commander put his pipe back in his mouth and lit a match. Slowly he puffed his tobacco back to life and ambled back to his desk and sat heavily down upon his chair. He leaned back, the chair creaking and moved the curtain of the window back a couple of inches and sighed.

"That idiot has gone?" the commander asked Klaus.

"Yeah, he took off snickering and running back toward the barracks." Klaus spoke softly.

The commander turned once more to Josef, again making firm eye contact. "I don't understand why you help the Jewish swine. I don't even care to know. I just know that I SHOULD have you hung for treason, which is exactly what some of these other notes from your other commanding officers say. They say you are a damn fine soldier, but misguided, obviously."

Josef felt Klaus's hand on his shoulder, gripping tightly. Everything in him wanted to grab the hand of his friend but he did not want to come across as a homosexual amidst all the other charges.

The old man cleared his throat and spent a long few seconds pulling on his mustache again.

"You're a damn fine soldier. You've got some fine credentials and despite the drivel that piss ant was saying a few minutes ago, I'm still promoting you to General. But listen to me closely young man! I'm tossing out the notes from your former commanding officers. If you fuck up again, it's on you...AND him!" The commander pointed at Klaus.

"You run your Jewish saving shit where I'm sending you and you're done! He's done too!" The old man motioned again toward Klaus with his pipe. "I only yelled about hanging you, because I too dislike that fool. About the time he runs around telling everyone you are dead. I'll tell him you've been promoted." The old Commander chuckled, as though imaging the shock on the face of the Lt that was nothing but a pain in his rear end.

After a momentary chuckle, he became deadly serious again, "I'm not letting you go free, I'm just sick of your current commanding officer in here every day complaining. I realize his complaints. They are real, at least some of them are, but I'm just getting sick of him bitching every single day. I'm simply giving YOU one single last chance and your friend here is going to pay the price if you fuck up again! You're too good of an officer to hang, so is he, but you are both too much of a problem for me here, I'm sick of it. Now get your ass on the train, Generals. Both of you. You're heading to Majdanek. You will report there in three days. Now get out of my sight."

Chapter 2

Another month had passed inside the camp. Seven months and one week now. Eva had been a good girl and hiding or at least being as unnoticeable as she could when an officer would walk past. Hanna had spent many days under the sun in the "caretakers" garden last summer and in the kitchens all the rest of the time. The only thing that had saved Eva was Hanna's own green thumb; well that and the relative quiet of the green house.

When they had first arrived last August, Hanna had watched as the lines of innocents had marched off the cars. She had watched children be ripped from the arms of their parents and she had cried. Fortunately for them both, she had waited inside long enough to be at the end of the quickly moving line.

When screams, cries, pleading and begging for simple human decency had failed, some of her fellow inmates were thrust into what was surely the killing line. That line had only elders, small children, some of the sickly or infirm and yet, some who seemed perfectly healthy. The Germans just chose however they felt like; Judge, Jury and executioner. Surely the other, shorter line was the line to get into.

She had strained to hear above all of the shouts and screaming why each group was being sorted. Above all the din, the screaming, the sounds of clubs raining on helpless victims, she heard a few words. "Doctor!" "Chemist!" "Scientist!"

That day, the line was drawing her ever nearer and she knew it was now or never. The stained concrete against the backdrop of electric fence and razor wire galvanized her to action. She had to get into the short line. She was convinced that was the way. As she had been somehow still able to keep her long dress coat, she had tucked Eva underneath.

"Don't say a word. Hold on to mother. Wrap your arms around in front. Step when I step!" She had wrapped her long coat around them both. Surely the SS would see that she had four legs.

The first two guards hit her on the shoulders; the next would have hit her back if they had not gone through her daughters back first. Little Eva never screamed out, just gripped tighter. Holding on to her mother; trusting that her mother was making the right decision. Hanna didn't even know if she was. She was just trying to make her girl survive, her baby had to live. She had choked back the tears and ran, cursing herself as her daughter's shorter legs struggled to keep up.

Hanna reached outside of her coat and held on to her daughter's shaking arms. She *had* to make it through. Her Eva's life depended on her decision right now.

"Halt!" Hanna stopped at the barked order. While she had watched other mothers disappear while hanging their heads in shame, a shame that was not theirs, Hanna turned her brown eyes to the guard and stood up straight. Softly, yet discreetly she squeezed her daughter's arms wrapped around her waist.

"I am a botanist! I can grow all of your vegetables and fruits!" She yelled as though she were confident, but her very insides were shaking. This was the moment, the moment where she would essentially meet her maker, or be thrust into what was surely the bowels of hell. Neither guaranteed life. Nothing could anymore.

The thick necked SS grabbed her arm and then the back of Eva's head. Although knowing it was likely going to get them both killed, Hanna swung around and put her fists up; prepared to fight to the death over her child. It was nothing new for the guard. Many tried. None were successful. It was only a simple irritation, and sometimes entertainment. The beef necked SS had glared at her, the short portly woman to his side stepped up with her baton in place to strike Eva.

The large SS guard grabbed the woman guards swinging arm. "Nien" this one belongs to me!" The round, bitch faced woman spat on his shoes and turned away.

The burly SS grabbed Hanna's arm and swung her around behind him, Eva barely hanging on swinging behind. He turned, yanked Hanna's coat open and grabbed the back of Eva's neck and shoulders from the oversize coat and pulled her out, as though holding on to a kitten. He held her at arm's length. Eva's eyes opened wide but she caught Hanna's stare and slight shake of her head. "No! Eva, No! Don't cry!" Hanna mouthed the words, hoping desperately her child understood and followed the advice.

Eva took a deep breath and as though the hand of God had touched her, she hung calmly in the grasp of the great brute's hand by the back of her neck. Eva crossed her arms and whispered ferociously, "You want to eat don't you? I'll fix your gardens!"

The SS brute tossed Eva to Hanna. "Shut her up and don't move!" Whether he liked to eat, he felt a slight twinge of human decency or he simply respected the young one's bravery, no one would ever know. But it didn't matter to Hanna, her baby would live. At least for today. Today Eva would live.

Without losing a stride he regained his place in line and began shoving the rest of the inmates into various lines.

"No! That's my friend! Hanna! Hanna! Eva!" The shrill scream echoed louder than the others. Hanna looked at her friend Marta she had met on the old, rumbling train car. They had shared many a story and surprisingly even a laugh or two on the way to Lublin, to Majdanek. To hell.

Hanna met her friend's frightened eyes. She couldn't let her friend die, but what would be the punishment for her and her daughter be if she spoke up? Hanna tore her eyes away from her new friend's gaze to stare towards the unforgiving ground. She pulled Eva to the front of her coat and curled around the small child. She hugged tightly, hoping that the child wouldn't hear Marta cry.

"Zahradník! Zahradník!" Marta screamed. Hanna quickly looked up and into her friend's eyes again. Had Marta heard her yell botanist? Had they talked about gardening? Hanna couldn't remember, but was too scared for her daughter's life to yell to her new friend.

It was killing Hanna to ignore Marta's crying, to stand by and do nothing. Just then the angry, oversized female guard grabbed Marta and shoved her alongside Hanna and Eva. "This one is mine. I like to eat too, pig!" The female guard spat once more and resumed her duties with the rest of the line of inmates, enjoying herself and her job.

Hanna, Marta and Eva had stood then. The rain turned from a mist into a heavy, cold, late spring downpour. Hanna tucked Eva beneath her coat and tried to shield the child from as much of the chilling spring rain as she could. She felt her daughter shiver, but there was nothing she could do to protect her anymore. Hopefully, she had made the right choice.

The last two inmates were shuttled off the train car. The large guard shoved them to the long line without as much as a glance, without conscience, as he had done for thousands. Turning his attention back to the small trio, he grabbed Marta by the hair and ordered Hanna to follow. Hanna ran to keep up, holding her daughter tightly against her side. She knew if she dropped Eva, or if Eva tripped that she would be gone forever.

The guard marched them to the end of a line of prisoners, "You're going through the disinfection, filthy swine. When you are done you are to come directly to me" he pointed his rifle toward a large office building near the front of the encampment. He scowled down at Eva, as if once more deciding what he was going to do with the child. Once more Eva surprised Hanna at her ability to read the guard. Eva scowled back at the guard, as best she could. For a five-year-old, she had a lot of spunk. The guard stepped up to Eva and pushed her down with the barrel of his rifle. Still the child didn't cry or make a sound, although she did quickly sit to avoid the hard, cold steel pressing into her ribs.

He pushed her once more and turned on his heel and marched off to the office building. So far, it had seemed that they had escaped. Hanna finally released the sigh and the tears she had been holding. There were other guards around, but none were actively watching them. Hanna and Marta embraced, not sure what perils were ahead of them, but knowing that somehow they had been spared. Eva scrambled to her feet and wrapped her small arms around Hanna. Eva's shaking shoulders bumped Marta's arm and the young woman reached a hand to the child's head. "Poor baby, I have always wanted my own, but today I am happy that I was never blessed with a beautiful child such as this poor babe."

Hanna lifted the child to her and together her, Marta and Eva walked into the foul smelling gloom of the cement barrack, to the shower area, not sure if they would ever come out again. Millions never would.

Chapter 3

Josef and Klaus had not spoken for the first part of their journey from Berlin to Lublin. The once close friends had retained an awkward politeness. Neither actively speaking to the other or making conversation, but politely answering each other's questions. Many times over their lives they had sat in silence next to each other; that comfortable silence that real friends can have. This time was different though. The stilted conversations today were just a simple echo from a lifetime of friendship.

What was there left to talk about? Josef knew he could never change what was in his heart. He hated the war, he hated the regime, yet he was one of the high ranking officers. It was the only way he could help. Once they had received their boarding passes and instructions, he found out he was promoted 'to second in command' at Majdanek until the current Commander moved on. He would be in charge of an entire concentration death camp. He was now in charge of this whole damn killing machine. He would give almost anything to not be in this new role. Doing nothing would be worse, running away would be worse still. He would not be able to help any should he run.

His fellow officers and the soldiers in his unit had bought him some of the best beers to celebrate. Hell, he had celebrated with them; he did get a great promotion. He and Klaus had left the office. Klaus had pulled him behind one of the closest buildings and yelled, "You stop this bleeding heart bullshit! I can't keep looking the other way; your shit is going to get me killed!"

After his yelling, as Klaus usually did, he went back to his old self and they had met at the mess tent and proceeded to get rip roaring drunk. Klaus had been promoted too. Majdanek was in a constant state of construction, and now even more prisoners were arriving. More innocent souls. Klaus and Josef were to equally share in the second in command position underneath Alfred Rissling.

Once he moved on to his new role, no one seemed to know exactly what that was; they were to take over the entire running of the camp.

At the party, they had laughed and bumped elbows with their friends. It was as if nothing had happened in the commander's office. At one point they had both bent over the table laughing at a game of cards, spilling some heavy foam over the Lt.'s head accidentally, of course. That piss ant had been pissed, but now that he was outranked, what could he have done? Nothing. And that's exactly what he did. As the night had worn on and the ale passed quickly, the tension between the two friends and soldiers began to become palpable. Now on the train to Majdanek, Josef wasn't sure if their friendship could ever be retained as it used to be.

He couldn't change what he felt in his heart. Always before, he could trust that Klaus would grudgingly look away, but he knew that was no more. The commander had made sure of that. He sighed and pulled a cigarette from his pack. Hitler abhorred smoking, and Josef found himself lost in his thoughts regarding the irony. Hitler hated smoking and the effects it had on the body, yet he found it perfectly reasonable to murder millions of people.

Klaus looked at his friend, his brother. He was pissed. He understood that Josef saw things differently, he didn't understand why of course, but he understood. Now his bleeding heart sympathy could get him killed.

"Dammit man! You couldn't have gotten us a promotion without trying to get us both killed, could you?"

Josef looked up at his friend and smiled; an apology on his face. "Guess not Klaus". His voice broke. He was, in his own rights, a prisoner too.

Klaus sat on the bench seat next to his friend, his elbows on his knees and looked down at the old plank floor. He sighed heavily, "Damn Josef. You're my friend. You know I'll do all I can to keep you from getting your pansy ass killed. You do the same for me all right?"

It wasn't an apology, nor was it a threat. It was however, more than Josef had expected and he was thankful to his friend for giving him that trust. He was actually amazed at how compassionate Klaus could be when he wasn't dealing with a Jew. Maybe Klaus was right, that there did need to be this purge. He just couldn't understand the inhumanity of it though. If it HAD to be done, couldn't it be done more humanely?

Josef smiled at his friend, Klaus punched him in the arm in return and ruffled his hair as he stood up. "Come on dumbass; let's get on with this promotion shit." Josef punched him back, "After you asshole."

Together the men grabbed their duffels and descended the stairs. At the bottom Klaus stopped. Thick black smoke, curled from a large chimney in the distance. The direction they were headed; the direction toward Majdanek. A faint, yet sickeningly sweet smell filled the men's nostrils. Klaus took a step back and into Josef. "Stop backing into me you faggot" Josef pushed him forward and stepped onto the platform still chuckling.

An SSPF was waiting to take them to Majdanek. The men noticed several other trucks parking close to the back of the train. Josef's suspicions were realized when the last two freight cars were opened and SS soldiers began throwing people into the waiting trucks. Men, women, children…they were all pushed and thrown, as though they were merely objects instead of the human beings that they were. Klaus watched for only a moment, a disinterested look on his face. Josef glanced and looked away, not wanting to watch anymore.

Both men tossed their bags into the waiting staff Steyr and climbed in the vehicle. Josef sat in the back. Klaus eased himself into the front seat. Josef noticed Klaus's knuckles go white around the handle of his bag and he looked up to see what Klaus was watching. A young boy who seemed to be about 10 or 11 had leapt from the truck and was running parallel with the train. Josef whispered under his breath, "Hide. Get under the train. Go!" Still the child kept running parallel with the long train. Running for his life, but not realizing he could not outrun an SS bullet.

Two SS on the dock casually brought up their rifles. They seemed to be in no hurry, this was obviously nothing new for the men. The young child's hair flew up and for just a split second, the blood created a light red halo effect as he came to a stop before falling face first into the mud, or at least what was left of his face. "Jesus Christ" Josef heard Klaus mutter.

"Jesus Christ is right! Did you see the lead they gave that kid? They almost let him get away! They shouldn't wait so long. What a game! Last week two of the pigs got away though." The SSPF laughed again, saluted the men who had shot the escaping child and turned the wheel heading from the station of death. They were headed to Majdanek.

The high fences and buildings stood directly in front of them, rust colored stains still on the cement at the entrance to the camp. .

"Oh damn, Josef! What the hell is that nasty, rank smell?" Klaus took a small step forward as he surveyed the surroundings at the gate of his new assignment. Majdanek concentration camp.

Josef clenched his hands but kept his arms tight on the duffel bag for an instant, then dropped it. He stepped in front of Klaus grabbed his uniform by the lapels and slammed him against a post at the entrance. A guard below saw this, turned on his heel and started towards them.

"The smell is what the hell I've been keeping those few people from. They're burning them alive, Klaus! What they don't burn, they just toss into piles…and then they LIVE in it!" Josef harshly whispered and slammed Klaus against the train one more time before letting go of him. Klaus shook his uniform out and glared at Josef, yet said nothing. The rumors they had heard were true.

The approaching officer smartly saluted, Klaus and Josef returned it. "Generals, SSPF Reeding at your service, if you will follow me." The thin pock faced officer did a quick about face and headed towards the office. Klaus elbowed Josef on the way past and followed the new SSPF. Still he said nothing.

The men walked into the dimly lit office and approached the desk. They saluted the young commander behind it. Arrogantly, the young commander stood and brushed off the bit of dust off his sleeve they had brought in with them and saluted them back lazily, arrogantly.

He sat back in his chair and picked at a manicured fingernail for a full 30 seconds before he turned to look at them again. "Well. Sit down you fools. I don't know why the hell you are here, and frankly I don't give a rat's ass. You're supposed to be my new second in command for a while until I leave this place."

Before the men could sit, the arrogant young commander began to pick lint off of his uniform. "Eva!"

A small girl about five or six peered in from behind the men with a large plate of sandwiches. She struggled to balance the weight of it and keep walking. Josef heard footsteps in the hallway and was sure that a benevolent someone had been there holding the tray and just passed it to the girl to carry into the room. The child walked to the desk and put the tray down.

"Haven't I told you to walk faster when I call you?" He jumped up, fist raised and quickly walked around the desk, stalking the young child. The shrinking girl backed up quickly and ended up between Klaus and Josef. She quickly went stiff and tilted her head backwards to look at them; her dark eyes and long lashes meeting Josef's blue grey eyes. In a surprisingly sweet and clear voice she whispered, "I'm sorry."

Josef took a step to the side and the slight, scared girl stumbled in between them and fell onto her rear directly on Klaus's right foot. He looked down and met her eyes. For a split second as he looked into her eyes, he saw a ghost from his past. His young sister had had the most startling beautiful brown eyes. They were unusual for his family, but beautiful just the same. Klaus was uncomfortable with the feeling he got from looking at the small girl. The little creature that was so much like his beloved Sonja was. It was a brief moment as their eyes met, but Klaus didn't want this officer hitting this child, not that he cared of course, he just wasn't in the mood for it now.

Gruffly he scolded the child, "Get off of my clean shoes" He pushed the trembling girl towards the doorway with a stiff leather boot and looked at the young commander.

"What is the plan then? What the hell are we doing here? Eating or just sitting on our asses waiting for you to tell us what to do" Klaus barked at the young commander.

Josef watched the Commander as he seemed torn. He obviously wanted to finish whatever he had planned to start with the poor girl before Klaus pushed her out of the room. The commander glared at Josef and Klaus then returned to his desk; his back stiff. He pulled two files from the stack and began to page through them. "You began as foot soldiers seven years ago" he said with disdain, as though fighting and watching men die that you knew was just something they decided to do for fun. He closed the files and cast them to the top of the pile, not caring.

"You might as take this plate of food with. I'm not hungry. Not after that Jew pig touched it. Eva!" The Commander yelled again, both men wincing at the shrill, nasally echo off the walls.

The girl in the short stained and yellowed dress walked into the door again and stood hesitantly just a few feet inside. "Take these men to building B. Carry their food and when you are done, don't come back. Stay out of my sight or I'll make you stay out of my sight. Or better yet, I'll keep you in my sight hanging from the gallows over there to show everyone else what will happen if you don't obey orders quickly and efficiently. DO YOU UNDERSTAND?" The quiet girl nodded solemnly and reached for the oversize tray.

"She'll take you to your office and quarters. It's raining like a sieve out there and I'm not going out in it." The Commander strode from his office with a dismissive wave and down the hallway out of sight.

Josef and Klaus looked at each other, "Foot soldiers" Klaus pantomimed nasally…

"It appears that way. Stupid ass."

CHAPTER 4

At the front door to the Commander's barracks Klaus looked down at the slight child, shaking from exertion already as she had her arms stretched around the plate as far as she could reach and ripped the tray from her hands. "We're never going to get anywhere if we have to wait for you to take us there holding this. Let's go!"

Josef spared a glance at his friend. Never one to lessen the burden on anyone, Josef found himself rather amazed. He found the girl looking up adoringly at Klaus. Klaus caught Josef's disbelieving stare. "Don't start with me, Josef. I don't want to hear a word of it." Klaus roughly shoved the girl toward the door of the barrack, though not as hard as he could have...he too had seen the girl's eyes on him.

The slight, dark eyed girl stumbled and ran to the door, opening it to the pouring rain outside. She pointed to a building on the other side of the courtyard. The men took off towards the building at a run with the small girl trailing behind in the cold rain.

Under the awning of the building the men stopped and watched as the youngster clambered up onto the deck. Her dark hair was slick on her head and her eyelashes looked even longer with the rain. She turned her somber eyes towards the door and walked into the new barracks for Josef and Klaus.

Klaus thrust the tray at her, "Think you can handle this now?" The girl nodded, took the tray and slowly carried it to the table. She stood next to the table afterwards and stared towards the men. They paid her no mind as they hung their uniform coats on the coat rack nailed to the wall.

"What the hell is up with that fancy pansy?" Klaus asked Josef

"I don't know I'm still stuck on 'foot soldiers'" Josef chuckled and pantomimed the young commander again.

The men grabbed their duffel bags and turned to find the young girl still at the table. She was facing them, but clearly her eyes were stuck on the plate of food in front of her.

Klaus snapped his fingers and the girl looked up guiltily. She held their gaze for a second before dropping her eyes to the floor where one dirty, small toe peeked through the top of her worn leather shoe.

Klaus walked over to the obviously hungry girl and knocked a sandwich off the tray and onto the floor as he went past her, trying to avoid coming into contact with her.

"Look what you did, you clumsy, silly girl! Pick it up and eat it over there in the corner. *Now*! Get out of my sight too!" He walked into the first room off the common area with his bag. Klaus found himself angrily throwing his clothes out of his bag and onto his bed, not even bothering to unfold or hang them. He was sure not being a pansy, it was just that that kid out there just reminded him of his sister Sonja.

His parents had thought they were all done having children when their youngest Klaus was about 10 years old. Sonja had been born a beautiful child, with the most unique doe brown eyes. Klaus, while a scrappy, rough and tumble boy, had delighted in spending time with Sonja. Sonja had been his whole world.

She had died when she was only five and he a teenager. He had been out with his friends and returned happy. He had picked her up a shiny rock to show her when they had been down by the river. She wasn't home when he got back. Klaus shook his head. So what if this scrappy, Jewish whelp looked like Sonja? She sure wasn't her…and never would be.

The girl had cringed for a moment expecting a slap, or worse as Klaus had walked on past but when nothing happened she slowly peeked out through her long, dark lashes and eyed the sandwich on the floor hungrily. She bent at the knees and squatted carefully beside the sandwich. She peered at Josef in the archway and looked back at the sandwich. When he made no move to stop her, she reached a small hand towards the sandwich. She pulled her hand back quickly at the creak on the old board and looked the other way.

"Did I tell you to pick it up or did I tell you to stare at it?" Klaus quickly walked over, picked up the sandwich and thrust it into the girl's hands. "Now get over there in the corner. You're dirtying up my kitchen."

The slight Eva ran to the corner. She turned and leaned her back against the wall and slowly slid down to rest on her small back side. She curled her legs in front of her and stared at the sandwich.

The men pulled chairs out by the table and ignored the small child. Klaus pulled a flask from his vest pocket and unceremoniously plunked it on the table beside the tray. Josef smiled, Klaus was back.

Taking a deep swig from the flask he passed it to Josef and then looked over to the girl. She was ignoring them and focused on splitting the sandwich into three equal pieces. She was so focused she didn't hear Josef's quiet footsteps until she noticed his shining boot just inches from her. She slowly walked her gaze up in his uniform and to his own light eyes.

He tossed another sandwich onto her lap. "I'm tired of watching you try to pull that sandwich apart like a busy chipmunk with way too much time on her hands."

She looked at him as a single tear rolled down her cheek. She quickly took a bite of the sandwich and smiled at him with bread crumbs on her lips. He waved his hand dismissively at her and returned to the table.

Klaus glared at him, but unusually for him, Klaus didn't say a word as he withdrew a candy bar from his vest pocket. Josef chuckled, candy and whisky and cigarettes were all stored near and dear to Klaus's heart. His friend had many vices.

Klaus was looking back on the events of today. He had seen many of the same things plenty of times before, but maybe what made it different was that this tiny girl being abused had a name. Eva. What difference a name made, he wasn't quite sure why, but he was glad he had stopped her abuse. Even if she was just a Jewish piglet, he simply just didn't feel like it today. That had to have simply been it. He had a hang over, he traveled on a shuddering train for hours and he just wasn't in the mood. The thought soothed him.

Why this particular child had affected him, he wasn't sure. He had seen and done much abuse himself. This child should be no different than any other. It was as though Sonja herself was in the room with him. Her light-filled persona; he could still remember all those years ago. He could feel Josef's eyes upon him, wondering at his actions. Klaus had never told Josef about Sonja, at least in how much the younger sister he had so briefly, had meant to him.

He bit off the candy bar and chewed thoughtfully. "I sure as hell am not saying you're right. You're still a dumbass, but I might be able to see a little bit more of your pansy ass reasoning now. What's the point in trying to beat a child? It doesn't make any sense. Just kill it and be done. That Commander," Klaus sneered nasally, pantomiming the commander "Is nothing but an idiot." He broke a small piece off the bar and turned to the girl, who was still comfortably sitting in his kitchen corner, "Hey kid! Catch" and tossed the small piece of chocolate towards the girl.

She picked up the small piece of chocolate next to her dirty shoe and carefully picked at it. "See what you made me do asshole? Now it's going to be like a dirty, mangy stray cat always following you around, getting tangled in your feet and yowling for something."

A small voice came from the corner, "No I won't Mister Kraus."

Josef tilted his head back and laughed. The first real laugh he had had in days. "Smart kid. I wouldn't follow your rank ass either."

"Shut up you bastard. What the hell do we do with it now? Toss it outside in the rain?"

Josef just laughed harder and took another swig from Klaus's flask. He had his brother back and he was happy about that. The question of the girl could be answered in time.

Chapter 5

Heavy footsteps followed by a loud knock filled the room. The girl quickly stood and shoved the sandwich pieces into her dress pocket and crossed her hands in front of her. Klaus nodded curtly and headed for the door. Josef put his index finger up to his bottom lip and lightly rubbed it. The girl's eyes widened and she reached up to wipe a crumb from her lip. Josef winked and stood.

The same young pockmarked soldier from the train stood holding an envelope, "Your orders, Generals." He handed the envelope to Klaus, saluted quickly and left the porch. A young woman in a striped uniform dress walked hesitantly toward the two new Generals. She carried a tray with a couple shot glasses and a bottle of German whiskey.

Klaus whistled and grabbed the tray. She didn't look half bad for a Jew whore, Klaus thought as he walked back to the table. Something familiar about the woman, but he couldn't place it. It didn't matter to him, just shocked that he felt a brief flash of recognition.

The woman did not move, but her eyes darted around the room as though she wanted to step inside and look around. Josef caught her gaze and looked back to Eva. "Eva!" The girl ran to the officer as quickly as she could without her sandwich pieces showing.

Josef gestured towards the woman; the little girl solemnly followed his gesture to land on the woman outside. Her face broke into a smile and she ran to the woman. The woman picked her up and squeezed her. The girl whispered into the woman's ear. The woman looked at Josef and cupped the child's head with her hand protectively. She gave a small smile and left the porch with a nod.

Hanna walked quickly with her daughter to the barracks they shared with many other women. Most of the women and children were 'new'. They hadn't been there long. Hanna shuffled in and rushed to the back of the barracks where their bunks were located. Their bunks were little more than a couple slabs of wood, but it beat sleeping on the floor…barely.

Hanna and Eva quickly sat down next to Marta. Marta lie on the bunk, exhausted. Marta worked in the guard's kitchen. She wasn't always a cook though. She was kept in a slightly better body condition than most of the other women in the camp. She was used terribly throughout the day and most of the nights. Eva handed Marta a piece of the sandwich she had saved, but Marta waved her away.

Hanna looked in to the bruised face of her friend, wishing she could do something, anything to help her. There was nothing she could do though, except hold her friends hand. She felt for her friend and wanted more than anything to help her, but she could not, lest she draw attention to herself and her young daughter.

There had been many times, she had walked in to find Marta cuddling her poor Eva rubbing her own weary hands over the fresh bruises on her girl's skin and wiping her tears away. The Commander in particular had a penchant for beating the girl. He never beat her hard enough to hurt or immobilize her completely, he took too much pleasure in torturing the girl to risk her not being able to come back the next day.

Hanna was lucky she did know her gardening, but wished her daughter had been able to help in the gardens as well. She hated her child being sent to be some jerks whipping boy for the day. Marta whispered to Hanna one night that the Commander, the sniveling, nasally jerk had been sick and in bed for a few days. She had been sent to his private quarters to see to his care and had found him in bed with another officer. He was gay.

Everyone knew the homosexuals were also on Hitler's kill list, but hardly any one of them were actually bad, as Hitler claimed they were. Some of course were criminals, as are segments of any society. What made the commander so horrible was that he was exactly what he took such great pride in destroying.

Those who had been dragged to his barracks, hoping their luck would change, were never seen again.

No one knew what happened, or spoke of it, but they all thought they knew. There was however, only one truth. Those men would never be seen alive again.

Marta groaned in her bed and rolled into a ball with her hands pressed tightly to her abdomen. "I'm dying Hanna. You have to get yourself and Eva out of here. I won't be able to help much more."

Hanna held her friends hand, "what do you mean? We are all dying Marta; all of us are dying a slow but sure death. I realize now that maybe we should have been in the other line. It would have been awful but for a few seconds, and none of this suffering would be our cross to bear."

"No Eva. You lived. You saved your baby. You saved us all. You made the right decision." Marta squeezed Hanna's hand. Her once rich auburn hair thin and almost brittle to the touch rubbed on Hanna's hand and Marta lay her head on Hanna's lap. Hanna squeezed her friends hand tightly.

"No. It is much better to live and have hope than it would be to have died with none. I am pregnant Hanna, by one of those soldiers in there. Soon I will be showing, and I will no longer be of use to any of them. Even the one who sired this poor little flower inside of me." She broke into heartbreaking sobs.

Hanna rubbed her friends hand with her thumb, while Eva stood on the bed and clung to her mother's neck. She didn't understand all of what was being said, but she knew enough not to say a word to anyone else, nor should she break up this embrace of two women caught in such a horrible trap as this place.

Eva patted her mom's head when she felt her mom begin to cry. "It's ok momma. We'll be ok in the end. That's what you always tell me."

"I know sweetness. It will be ok. Somehow, someway it will be ok. It has to."

"Bullshit!" the woman on the bunk next to her yelled, "It's never going to be all right! We're all going to die and you keep prolonging it with your bullshit stories! You're NOT going to get rescued. You are going to die in this prison. We are all going to die in here!"

Eva bent and buried her head under her mom's chin. She didn't like this woman who always yelled. Momma had called her a shrew and several of the other inmates had said her husband had probably paid to get away from her. It was a terrible joke. It was a joke that didn't make a lot of sense, nor was it even all that funny but they had all laughed, happy that even for a second they could picture a withered old man being harped at day and night and making a clandestine deal with the Nazi's just to be rid of this horrible woman.

No. It wasn't the least bit funny at all, but laughing in any form was a bittersweet, rare occurrence.

The woman yelled again, "There is no hope. Stop telling that baby there is, filling her head with nonsense."

Marta sat up on her bunk. "Leave the child alone!"

The woman, no one had bothered to learn her name, kept scolding. "You're better off to just let her go to sleep. There is too much pain here. She doesn't need to go through it anymore, Hanna. You are being selfish. She watches people die of starvation and worse every single day. How can you be any kind of a mother and put your child through that!" The woman's voice rose in pitch until she was screaming. "Kill the child yourself and spare her the agony of what is to come! You are a selfish, selfish woman!"

Eva ducked down behind her mom and friend. Both Marta and Hanna gasped, Marta leapt out of her bunk to the woman's side. Marta jumped on the older woman and grabbed her shirt collar.

"No, she's not being selfish. YOU are! Leave them alone!" Marta pushed the older cranky woman back down on her bunk.

The woman sat and arrogantly looked up into Marta's face. Slowly she stood until she was nearly nose to nose with Marta. She spat in Marta's face and then slapped her. "Want to talk about selfish? Look how fat they keep you, just to fuck you. We all know you're pregnant; they'll just have a bit more fun, sport with you some more for their carnal pleasures and then off you'll go! Poof!" The old woman slapped her hands together, emphasizing her point, "You're a whore; don't speak to me with your fake high handed bullshit. You're nothing more than a whore. You probably never were."

Marta leaped onto the woman and began to throw punches. Hanna set Eva down on the bed and jumped up to leap to her friend's side, but she heard the running of the SS Guards feet toward the entrance. She sat back down quickly and averted her eyes. The rest of the inmates did the same, as they all pretended no interest. A guard might see them staring and figure they had something to do with it, and they would pay whatever penalty the guard decided to dish out that day. They still might, no matter that they were not a part of it at all.

The punishments were never the same. For a fight, the whole barracks might not eat for a few days. Or if the guard was feeling magnanimous that day he might just ignore it and wait for the outcome. One never knew and the inmates had learned quickly not to intervene, lest they be charged with upsetting the "peace" as well.

The large door swung open and two guards came in. A young blond man of about 25 and an older, dark haired and mustached man of about 50 stood over the fighting women and watched for a couple minutes. The older woman had Marta pushed to the ground on her back and was straddling her. Marta's dark hair was haloed around her head. Both the old woman's bony hands were tight against Marta's neck, red and purple outlines of bruises already beginning to form on her neck, outlined around the tightly gripped fingers of the old woman.

The older woman leaned over more, her hips and legs moving up from Marta's abdomen to her ribs and breasts. Marta's thin dress rode up until her underwear and the slight curve of her stomach that hid the child within was showing. A younger SS stepped forward, pulled his pistol and shot the older woman on the side of the head. The wound stayed clean for just a second and then blood started with first a trickle and then a steady, pulsing flow down the side of her face. Slowly she released the hold on Marta's neck and slid off sideways.

The SS who shot the woman looked down at Marta. The older guard stepped forward and kicked the dead woman's legs off of Marta. He looked at Hanna and Eva and pointed his pistol at them and took a step forward.

"What happened here?" The barked command was not so much a question as an order.

Hanna stood slowly, carefully and answered, "The older woman went crazy and attacked the younger woman."

The younger SS yanked Marta to her feet and slapped her face a few times. "You will not eat for three days for this foolish behavior. You will report to my barracks in 10 minutes. If you do not arrive in that time, I myself will kill you for this action. Do you understand?" He shook Marta again and she nodded, barely coherent. He dropped his arms from Marta's shoulders and watched her waver in front of him.

The Guards turned as one to leave. They walked out the door and down the side of the building, toward the far end where Hanna, Eva and Marta slept. The older man chuckled, and said quietly "Lucky you pulled that angry guard stunt with me. You try pulling that over with anyone else, and they'll kill you. You have to be careful Jonah! This isn't the place to do that shit. I know that baby is yours, so will a lot of other folks as soon as they notice her showing. That gives you two weeks, Jonah. If it's not taken care of in two weeks, I'll kill her for you. Because I like you, I'll make sure it's quick. I won't let her go through the hall."

Chapter 6

Hanna listened intently, but the men walked away and the younger man's response was not heard. Hanna rushed to her friend's side and helped her sit down. She was torn, if she delayed Marta from going to the barracks she would be shot tonight. There would be no more pain for her, but it would mean Hanna herself had a hand in her own dear friend's murder. Surely it would simply be called a mercy killing and no one would know?

Except herself, she would know. She couldn't sabotage her friend's life, even to help her. She pulled Marta's head to her own chest and held her as the seconds counted by. What could she do? Marta only had two weeks to live anyway. She couldn't tell Marta what she overheard, could she? If she did, wouldn't that harm her more than not knowing? If the guard did keep his word to the young soldier, Marta would never know...alive one second and not knowing anything the next. Surely that would be the best for Marta?

Hanna pulled herself together and stroked Marta's hair, softly combing it down the best she could. She would make sure Marta made it to the young officer's barracks on time. In the meantime, she had two weeks to see if there was anything else she could think of to help her unfortunate friend. She braced herself and pulled Marta back to standing. She was getting her friend to the SS guard. He might have sinister plans for her friend, but the eavesdropped conversation seemed to point away from that. It was her hope. It was Marta's hope. She would deliver her friend herself.

Hanna pointed to the bed, bidding her Eva crawl in it and stay. Eva nodded and curled into the bed as far as she could. Hanna gave her a small smile and turned toward the door. "Marta, let's go. We've got six minutes left; you've got to walk with me." Marta groaned but leaned into Hanna and slowly began to put one foot in front of the other. The other inmates looked away as they walked past. Sometimes looking away from another's shame or pain was the only thing...the nicest thing that one could do.

As the women reached the door, another guard walked in to look at the dead woman. The guard sneered at Marta and Hanna, "Whores!" he shoved them both against the wall and groped Marta, "too bad that dumb kid won you in that last poker game, I could add some fresh bruises to your ugly face" He shoved Marta and watched as she fell sideways, still not aware enough to catch herself. He kicked her legs into the wall and walked further into the women's barracks. "You!" He yelled to the three women who were standing at the far end of the building. "Drag that dead bitch to the crematory now."

The women hastened to follow his order, the youngest pausing just for a moment to meet Hanna's eyes with a sorrowful look. The guard walked out of the barracks, pausing only momentarily as Marta struggled to sit up. Hanna pulled her friend to her feet and began the walk to the younger guard's barracks. She had three minutes to get her there now. She pulled Marta along as she began to jog slowly. She would make it, she had to make it.

Hanna knocked on the door. The young officer roughly grabbed Marta and pulled her inside, he motioned for Hanna to step inside and close the door. Just as Hanna reached the door handle to close it, the guard slapped Marta's face hard while twisting Marta's arm behind her back, making her cry out in pain. A laugh and guffaw from the other side of the dirt 'road' assured the young guard that the others knew Marta was in for a nice romantic torture lesson tonight. The assembled guards walked off as Hanna closed the door.

She turned and watched as the young guard tenderly lifted Marta into his arms and walked her to his bedroom. He came out a few minutes later and strode quickly across the room to Hanna.

He grabbed her by the throat, and at once, his almost boyishly handsome face turned into the face of what she could only describe as the face of a monster. His teeth showing, he nearly growled at her, "You mention what just happened to anyone between Marta and I, that pretty little daughter of yours is going to grow up real fast, but she'll die real slow! I'll make sure of that! You got it, bitch?"

Hanna nodded the best she could with his large hand at her throat. He pulled the door open and shoved her through it, slamming it behind her. She flew the three feet to the end of the porch and fell hard off the step onto the hard packed dirt below. While it was only a few feet high, it still knocked the wind out of her.

As she slowly pushed herself to her feet she heard soft footfalls head to the back of the barrack bedroom and smiled behind her hair. The young guard was going to Marta. Marta would be ok tonight, Hanna made the right decision. Her smile wavered when she remembered that Marta only had two weeks. Hopefully those two weeks would pass if not blissfully, then at least not painfully for her friend. She wondered if she would ever see her again.

Hanna began the walk back to her own bunk. Not sure what to do with her dear friend, or if there was anything she could do anyway. She walked quickly, hoping not to draw any attention to herself. Most of the guards knew what she was doing, but there were always a few that just couldn't seem to pass up the opportunity to assail anyone they wanted too, for any reason they could think of; real or imagined.

Chapter 7

A few men and women of the village gathered under the blacksmiths old roof. To make sure they did not attract any attention from the rest of the town's folk, the smithy, Henryk continued his work. The hammer ringing off the anvil in short bursts, then a blessed silence broken only by the old wheel of the forge breathing air into the fire.

"We have to do something. If even we save just one single soul, we have to try!" Henryck shouted, his lips barely noticeable beneath his large beard.

Another man agreed, "You realize that this will be found out one day. The world will know. Should we have them know we stood by and did nothing, or should we at least try? Do you have any idea how poorly those in the rest of the world will look upon us, every day walking past that camp and doing nothing?" The man shouted passionately, his voice rising in pitch along with the ringing anvil.

Another man stepped forward out of the gloom of the back of the smith's shop. He raised a hand to the men as though to stop talking long enough for him to speak. None of the men stopped their talking, or even acknowledged and the man stood by awkwardly.

Finally, a woman in the back row spoke up, "Hey! Antone Lienschoff is trying to say something!"

As one, the members of the community group huddled under the blacksmiths roof turned to watch the man they knew as Antone Lienschoff. The assembled people very nearly uttered a group sigh. No matter what endeavor they found themselves on, Lienschoff was sure to break in with some opposite view. The entire village knew he thrived on "stirring the pot".

No one ever admitted it, but each was sure that others in the group just wanted to toss Lienschoff right over the wall into the Nazi camp. The only reason anyone didn't was because Lienschoff had a big mouth, an arrogant attitude and was about as trustworthy and affectionate as a feral dog. Which was the only reason he was here at this clandestine meeting; it fell into the old adage, keep your enemies closer.

It was better to know what he was thinking; and you could tell exactly what he was thinking just by the look on his face. The few villagers decided that it was best to have him attend the quick meeting; thereby being culpable and just as likely the rest of them to be implicated, should the need arise to remind him of that fact.

"I say we don't do anything. The entire village is against this! No one wants to go in and offer ourselves to be murdered to save the life of one of them!" His face began to become redder as he spoke, "It's us or them! Leave them be! If you save one, all the rest will try to come pouring in, and where will that leave us? I don't like what they are doing. I don't like guns! And I don't like any of us getting involved in something that doesn't concern us!"

"Doesn't concern us? Those people are human! Just like us! They don't deserve to be killed and tortured and raped...." The Henryk's voice rang out, much as his hammer on his anvil did. Then his strong voice broke, "They...they're killing them... everyday, Antone! You know they are! Still you would have us sit on our asses and watch them! Grow a backbone man! They're killing babies, and you don't see a problem with that! What kind of a human are you?"

The blacksmith ended his rare speech with his hands on his anvil. His muscular shoulders bent, as though worn from exertion, but everyone knew how much that impassioned speech had cost the smith. His own son had been tortured and murdered by the regime, for simply looking too long into the confines of the camp on his way past.

The young man, the only son of the blacksmith, had been charged with conspiracy. The irony of the young man's death was that while his father was absolutely against the Nazi regime, his youngest child, now gone...had believed in the entire regime. The blacksmith turned to the face of his wife as she placed her hand on his shoulder and squeezed; a small bit of support in such a dire situation. She faced the gathered crowd and he stepped away from his anvil to allow his wife to speak.

He might privately give her hell over her nonstop "yammering" and yelling, but when it came down to it, he was proud to watch her take her place at his anvil and address their people.

Her eyes directed towards the sole nay-sayer of the group, and she called him out, without reservation or fear, "Antone, the *entire* village is *not* against this. If it were the case, there would be none of us here and all the rest of you folks, especially you Antone, would be somewhere else conspiring against us. My husband is right. Sooner or later, the rest of the world will find out what is happening here, and a large majority of them are going to blame us, alongside the Nazi's, because WE are letting it happen!"

Antoine with his greying, yet still fiery red hair stepped forward, "NO! It's too dangerous! You're just going to get people killed. This isn't up for discussion; we cannot and will not do this!"

A murmur among the men assembled went up. Antoine continued, "WE are not doing anything wrong! To save one is to sentence us all to death. Are you all too ignorant to know this?"

Beatrice, just as burly as her blacksmith husband hammered hard on the anvil. "Enough of this you dimwit! We're going to rescue some of those poor people, or we'll die trying. The world at large will find out about this and I'm not going to let it go down in history that we sat back and let it happen."

Antone stood as tall as his 5'5" could muster, "NO! You are spouting drivel! You're just doing this because your son is dead and you want some kind of sick revenge and you plan to use our village to do so!"

The large, bearded Henryk headed toward Antone with a snarl on his face, several men jumped between as Antone scrambled backwards. The blacksmiths wife banged the hammer on the anvil.

"Mayor! Would you be so kind as to shut this fool up inside the jail compound for a while? Keep him away from the other inmates, there won't be visitors of course, but should there be, don't allow them in. Let's see how Lienschoff likes being imprisoned like those poor folks at the "camp"."

She turned once more to the townsfolk in her husband's shop. "Men, and ladies, we are heading off to do what no one expects. We are going into that camp and no matter what; we are going to save some people! We can't let those poor people die, while we sit by and ignore every moral piece of humanity we possess. We might die. We might bring the very wrath of Satan upon us. Those who don't want to, go away now with our blessing, but respect us all enough to stay silent."

Beatrice took a step back from the anvil and stood, meeting each assembled village person in the eye. Everyone stayed. They would save some of those poor people.

Chapter 8

Klaus and Josef had spent a few weeks in what Josef called hell and Klaus called 'a stinking cesspool'. Either way described it perfectly.

Josef woke again to the noise of footsteps up to his door. He heard the door creak open and shut and Klaus's boots on the floor. Klaus was apparently up early. Hard to believe from the amount of spirits he had chugged down the night before. Klaus had been in a bad mood all day, bitching at everyone who had crossed his path. Inmates and guards; none of them had been safe from Klaus yesterday.

Josef lay awake for a few more moments. It was the end of April and even though some of the days got down right hot and humid, sometimes the mornings held a bit of a chill in the air. Josef sighed and forced himself out of bed. He pulled on his pants and grabbed his shirt off the chair. Another day loomed ahead, full of death and hatred and so much pity. He had to figure out what to do to help someone. All of them…but there was nothing he could do to ease their suffering. He, and his kind had done this to them. He was nothing short of a monster himself in here.

He had, well, they all had heard that Soviet forces were closing in on the camp, but they were still miles and months away at best. There was no reason to worry yet. Josef shook his head and sighed again as he finished buttoning up his shirt. If only he could be as emotionless as Klaus seemed to be sometimes.

Klaus looked up with red eyes as Josef stepped into the small kitchen. He pushed a glass of lukewarm and overly strong coffee towards Josef as he sat at the table. The two men sat in silence; there wasn't anything to say to each other now. What could they say? Any conversation up until this point seemed to turn into an argument. Josef was sure that Klaus was beginning to see things his way, and how utterly inhuman and wrong this whole camp was- No! The whole regime! His entire brainwashed country! Josef was turning back and forth. He knew it was wrong, but if it had to be, why couldn't it be more humane? There was no humanity in this camp from nearly all of the guards, and he was in charge of it all. He was Satan himself.

Klaus took a drink of his piss warm coffee and slowly stood. "I'm heading to the headquarters" He paused, "Took that mangy kid back to her ma last night. Commander beat the tar out of her. Guess she was too slow in helping his incompetent ass again."

Josef watched as his friends back as he walked out the door. He had heard of how bad the child had been beaten but fortunately had not had to see how bad it actually was. Several of the men had been laughing over a late dinner about it. "Swinging like a rag doll" and "damn Jewish piglets" were the talk of the night. He couldn't fathom why no one spoke out of this injustice, it wasn't right…and there wasn't a damn thing he could do about it.

He couldn't speak up, but was a bit surprised when some of the guards said nothing either. Jonah and Heinrich sat and said not a word. They were not unkind men. They were quick to shout and to land a few blows to a non-vital area if they were pushed to it, but they never went out of their way to purposely hurt those they were in charge of.

Yet then again, none of them could say anything, lest they be on the other end of the punishment. Everyone knew a former Nazi, or an outspoken German would be punished sometimes more severely than the Jews and others they already had imprisoned.

He was glad however that Klaus had brought the child back to her mother. He knew Klaus could be a brute, but he also knew that he hadn't harmed the child on the way back.

He took another small drink off his coffee and threw the cup in the sink. He pulled on his boots and walked out into the sunshine of the April morning.

Even though many weeks had passed since they had arrived, the foul stench of the camp was still a surprise to him every single morning he walked out. Several inmates walked past carrying a stretcher with another dead body on it. Their skin stretched tight over ribs and hipbones, they looked in poorer condition than the deceased they were dragging, and yet they were still walking. An older man in the front of the stretcher met Josef's eyes. His dark eyes on Josef's own blue eyes, it felt as though the old man could see into his very soul. Uncomfortable with the scrutiny, Josef turned his head away from the scene and began walking toward the command center.

"I don't give a shit what the hell you do to the pigs!" Klaus's voice rose above the din of the camp, waking up for another day in hell.

"Then I don't understand why you are still here bitching at me then" came the nasally and shrill voice of Rissling.

Josef stood below the step into the barracks to listen some more. Klaus's voice rose once more, "I don't give a shit what you do to the pigs; I just don't see why *you* have to beat up children just to prove your manliness…unless you are actively *trying* to prove it?" Klaus let his barb hang in the air and Josef walked up the step and into the command center.

Rissling was red faced, almost cowering in the corner. Josef took a hard look at the commander and his shaking hands. The man was terrified of Klaus; with good reason. Klaus was one bad guy to get into a fight with and he was just needling this ridiculous ass. No matter what Klaus's words actually said, what he was saying came through loud and clear, "Let's go!" No one wanted to fight with Klaus, not even Josef, even though they were pretty evenly matched. The Commander watched as Josef entered and stuttered, "Ge- Get out of my office."

Josef took a menacing step towards the Commander, "I don't know what you guys are arguing about, but you are out of here next week and we are in charge…unless you want to never leave. I'm sure that could be arranged too."

The Commander sneered at them when he heard feet approaching, sure that a fellow officer would be coming to assist him and these two men would get what was coming to them. Josef had heard the footsteps too and never worried about it. After being a soldier for so many years, he and Klaus both were tuned into more details than the Commander ever was or would be. Josef recognized the softer sound of a woman's feet on the hall outside and stood aside so she could enter.

Hanna entered and glared at the man who had dared abuse her child so terribly. She would never know what happened or what in her "snapped", but seeing the man who so abused her child and used her for a punching bag standing there she couldn't take it anymore.

Hanna felt her fists tighten up while heat in her face rose as the anger in her heart at her hopeless situation and this terrible man built up inside her. She screamed and ran towards the commander, her hands outstretched, as though ready to tear him limb from limb. She certainly wanted too. She ran past Josef but as she passed Klaus he whirled and grabbed her in his arms. With one hand he grabbed a handful of her hair at the back of her head and stopped her as quickly as though he had punched her in the gut.

He pushed her towards the door, his hand still holding her hair. At the doorway he shoved her out. She nearly careened into the wall opposite the door. "Get out of here and never rush toward an Officer again? You understand? Now get our breakfast on the table."

Klaus turned back to the Commander, not wanting to keep his back turned on him for too long. Josef looked at Hanna and saw the hatred on her face for Klaus. She looked as though she were ready to pounce on his back and start clawing at his face. Josef took a step towards her and met her eyes. Didn't this silly woman know that Klaus had just saved her life...even if it if had only been accidentally?

He stood firm, ready to grab her if she kept acting as though she were going to attack Klaus. He understood her pain, at least a bit, or he thought he did. He didn't have children of his own, but he could understand her pain none-the-less. He just wished she could understand that even though Klaus had seriously man handled her, that he did it- if even accidentally and saved her life. Had she actually attacked the ridiculous commander she would have been killed for it. As it was, she still could be killed if anyone else walked in right now and the nasally commander started whining about her actions.

He watched as the angry tears formed in Hanna's dark eyes. Her eyes brimming and her slight chest heaved from keeping her tears and her sobbing tightly inside her. After what seemed like a very long moment of silence, Hanna left the room and headed to the kitchen. Josef turned back to Klaus and the Commander.

The Commander remained in the corner with Klaus standing firm in the center of the room; his jaw clenched as tightly as his fists. The small windows let some of the spring sunshine in. Dust motes still swirled around in the air, sparkling with an innocence that was not to be found anywhere else in this horrible place.

Chapter 9

Hanna walked into the kitchen, her eyes still brimming with unshed tears. How terribly angry she was and how much she hurt for her baby; her poor brave Eva. She had wanted to gouge that villain's eyes right out of his head with her bare hands. Her scalp still hurt where Klaus had yanked on her hair. Of course, *he* would protect that horrible man. They were all the same. Klaus was a terrible person for obviously standing on the other side of right.

That Josef too! He was just as bad, maybe even worse! How dare he glare at her, like she was in the wrong! Then he just stood there, and didn't do a thing! Klaus had brought Eva back, barely conscious and covered in bruises! He had just unceremoniously tossed her on the bunk without a word or sparing a glance back. Of course, he had to have told Josef, and there that Josef was standing there glaring at *her*. Glaring as if she should thank him!

Had she not been half starved, no…more than half starved and it were a different time and place, she might have even found Josef to be pleasing to the eye. Right now though, any man who had muscles and more than an ounce of fat on his body was just another thing to show off the unfairness of a world gone mad.

She grabbed potatoes from the bin and began to slice them angrily on the counter. She took a moment to look at her hands, remembering how proud she used to be of her jewelry, her old wedding ring and her beautiful nails. Now her fingers were barely more than bones and her once beautiful fingernails were nothing more than ragged nubs on the end of her fingers. She couldn't stop the tears from falling any more than she could stop the pain in her heart, or the death that surrounded them all.

She slowly brought a shaking hand to her mouth and tried to stifle the sobs that she couldn't contain. How she hated this life, those horrible people in the office and what she had been reduced to. The world was no longer this safe and beautiful place, it was just a horrible, awful place to be. She stopped cutting the potatoes when the tears filled her eyes, she couldn't see.

She grabbed a large pan and started some water flowing into it. Maybe while she waited for the water to run into her pan, she could start to collect herself. She braced both hands on the sink in front of her and let her head fall to her chest. It was hopeless.

There wasn't any brave rescuer coming, there wasn't this massive allied army ready to roll in with tanks and guns and stop all this horrible stupidity. There was only her. Alone and trying to raise a baby in the pits of hell. Maybe some of the women were right and she was being selfish trying to keep her Eva alive in here, inside hell. Surely death could come quickly enough that the few moments of pain or panic wouldn't be nearly as awful as this slow death sentence was.

Right now, Eva had only been hurt physically. No one as of yet had been perverted enough to take what little innocence her dear girl had left.

A soft creak of a floor board had her spinning around. Josef stood in the doorway. As much as she had hated him a few moments ago, glaring at her, she hated it even more that he stood in the doorway with a pitying look on his face. How dare he pity her! He and his kind were the reason she was in here at all! His kind was the sole reason she was here, and thousand around her died every single day!

She turned back to the sink and turned the water off and began to cry in earnest as she reached for her kitchen knife and another potato.

Her fingers fumbled and she dropped her potato on the floor. Her heart felt as though it would shatter into a million pieces. She fought to control her sobs once more as she bent to pick it up. A soft sound from her right side and she looked up to see Josef holding out her potato to her. This one small act of kindness almost hurt worse than all the months of pain and suffering. She couldn't see to take it out of her hand, so he carefully placed it on the counter in front of her and walked away.

Tomorrow night, Hell be damned, she was getting out of here! She had heard rumors of a small hole in the fence and some villagers on the other side. If she could get to that tonight, even just to push her small daughter under it…she was going to do it. Her baby would live. It mattered not anymore if she didn't….but her baby had to. She HAD to live! Eva would survive!

Josef slowly turned from the kitchen and walked back to his barrack. He knew she was hiding something in those hazel eyes; he just wasn't sure exactly what. Her brimming eyes and the pain so deep cut him to the quick. There just wasn't anything he could do. Couldn't she see and understand that? What did she expect him to do? Take on the entire German army on his own? Or worse yet amass a ragtag band of half dead prisoners and attempt it then? Didn't she understand?

Maybe he'd sleep on it tonight and see if there was anything he could even think of doing to save that girl and her incredibly courageous mother.
It had hurt him to be so rude to her; he could only imagine her pain at seeing the man who had hurt her daughter so much.

Chapter 10

Klaus left the Officer's porch. He had turned his back to Rissling and walked out angrily. He sure as hell didn't care about any Jew-ling, but he had heard about Rissling's odd behavior, and he had never liked people like him anyway. People who hated their own, judged their own and condemned their own.

Klaus cleared his throat as he walked towards the main barracks for the women. He wasn't checking on the kid, obviously, but he did have to make sure her other bunkmate, the whore, was working and not sitting around on her ass watching the dumb kid sleep.

He stepped into the gloom of the dark windowless barracks and held his breath. No matter how often he had to step inside, he never could get past the horrible smell. Even after he left any of the barracks and took a hot shower, he still felt as though he could taste the rancid smell of death. Of sickness and squalor.

He walked back to the corner where he knew the child was. He didn't see her in the corner right away, his eyes hadn't yet adjusted when he heard the small whimper, much as a baby animal might make.

He stood a moment as his eyes adjusted and looked at the small form on the wooden platform. He didn't feel pity, he never felt pity...so he couldn't put into thoughts what exactly he was feeling. He just didn't like it. He told himself that was all. He simply didn't like it.

When the small object of his musing turned her head and looked up at him he felt himself inexplicably drawn to her. After taking a quick and careful look around to make sure no one, especially one of Rissling's cronies saw him, or worse, Josef *the cry baby* saw him, he knelt towards her bunk.

"Hi Kraus. I'm tired"

"Yeah"

His wealth of small talk used up, Klaus began to stand to walk away. There was nothing for him here. He honestly didn't even know why he was here. He looked at the rest of the barracks as he stood and turned back at her voice.

"Did you come to check on me, Kraus?" The slight voice wavered a bit from the pain in her bruised ribs as she turned to face him, her eyes so much like his younger sisters.

"Don't be stupid. Of course I didn't. You are Für mich nicht wichtig! I just walked through to make sure all you are where you're supposed to be. I'm just doing my job." He said gruffly. She *was* of no importance to him! She never would be!

"Oh."

Klaus muttered under his breath as he strode away. He stopped, but refused to turn around and face her when he heard Eva's voice through the dark barrack.

"Thank you"

He strode out the door without answering her. A Waffen did not accept accolades from a Jewish brat. He stepped into the light of the day and ducked back inside the room to the right of the door when he saw Rissling headed past with another officer.

Klaus quietly listened as the men walked past. "Sure I could have kicked his ass for talking back to me, but there was no reason too. I leave this place in a while, no reason to bother with a fool like Klaus." Rissling's nasally voice inflected on his name. "*Klaus.*"

Klaus almost rolled his eyes as he listened to Rissling brag. When the men had passed, Klaus walked out and off to his duties; the girl seeming to be forgotten.

Deep in the darkness of the barracks, Eva curled up and closed her eyes. Her soft breathing was the only sound in the building. She smiled as she fell into a deep sleep. Kraus wasn't a monster. He came to check on her. He was the stupid one. Momma said he didn't care about anything, but she knew.

Klaus liked her, but he wouldn't ever tell anyone. Klaus was her friend even if he didn't want to be. She smiled again and fell headlong into a sleep that would last long into the next afternoon. She liked Klaus. He reminded her of someone, but she couldn't remember who exactly. Someone young, with a quick smile who had been her friend for a short time, long ago.

Chapter 11

Josef watched as Rissling and his idiot friend walked past the barracks and was preparing to head into the women's area where Eva was when he was startled by Klaus walking out.

"Let her sleep" was all Klaus said as he walked out into the fresh air and took a deep breath. It still stank out here, but wasn't as bad as the stagnant, nasty air inside the bunk room.

Josef nodded and walked away to his duties. The day would pass slowly, more would die and he would be helpless to stop it.

His heart heavy, he walked slowly across the muddy road to his cabin. Back to his friend and his bottle of whiskey; anything to numb the pain. He stopped and stood at the corner of his barracks and looked up at the stars, just beginning to twinkle innocently over his place in hell.

He watched his breath puff out from his hurting body and grimaced at his earlier thoughts. What right did he even have to think about his own suffering? He was surrounded by the worst suffering that any human culture had ever thought of, let alone do. He was on the other side of it. The side that wasn't dying by the thousands daily and here he was out taking a stroll kicking rocks and complaining. He sighed from deep in his chest. Even that hurt and he chastised himself again.

"She's got you, doesn't she; that little girl?" Klaus walked out of the shadowed porch and towards Josef. He pulled deep on the cigarette in his lips and the end glowed red, casting an almost eerie glow over his face.

Josef said nothing, just sighed again and shook his head no before lowering it to stare at the ground. There weren't words for what he was feeling. Klaus must have thought so too. He abruptly turned away and walked in the door. After a moment Josef turned and put his foot on the step. He bumped into Klaus who was putting a glass of golden whiskey in his hand.

"Drink up. I will too. There isn't anything to talk about tonight, Josef. Your damned bleeding heart crusading and moping around is irritating me."

Josef looked up at his friend on the porch. While anyone else in hearing distance might think Klaus was angry, Josef knew different. Klaus would never say of course, but he too was feeling the strain and perhaps even some of the pain that he himself was feeling.

They were trapped, as surely as the poor souls they were sent to lord over were trapped. The only difference was they had food. Josef put his hand on the railing and swallowed the contents of the shallow glass. They stood for a long moment and as one, went inside their barracks.

Several days had passed and Rissling was getting bored. It was too long alone, and he still had no Eva to torture. He was getting tired of being here, and he was damn tired of Klaus and Josef always jumping in his way.

They never did anything wrong, per say, but it seemed as though they delighted in constantly thwarting whatever he planned. Today though, he would order that Eva be brought to him. His room had a need of cleaning and watching her walk around stiffly with his marks of brutality on her had a certain ring to it today. He was bored and she was a good brand of entertainment.

He stepped outside of his barracks to find a messenger and saw none other than Eva trailing along behind Josef toward his barracks.

"What the hell are you doing?" Rissling shrieked and marched off his porch towards Eva and Josef.

Josef walked towards Rissling, effectively shielding Eva from Rissling's view. "I needed a worker, and couldn't find an available one, so I picked this runt up to finish the cleanup work in my barracks." Josef firmly answered the man.

There was nothing Rissling could say, Josef and Klaus were the ones effectively running the camp anyway with Rissling uncaring, knowing he was out as soon as his paperwork was in.

Rissling bristled. Of course, Josef would just come out of nowhere and once again mess up his plan for the day. Josef always foiled all of his plans! Ever since day one and they had purposely stopped him from wailing on that dumb kid!

The girl was supposed to be his entertainment for the day. He purposefully set aside time just to torment the child in his day. Now there she was casually walking off with one of the men he hated!

He would make her pay somehow. Her face didn't show anything, but Rissling knew she felt smug as she walked away from him. Almost as though she knew she had a benefactor. He could all but feel the little shit laughing at him. In truth, Eva felt none of those things, with the exception of one. One that Rissling never even considered.

Josef would protect her. She could feel it. He never told her that, and she knew he wouldn't ever tell her. Yet, he had carefully helped her out of her bunk and helped her put her shoes on, because she hurt too much to do it herself. His touch had been like the Papa that she barely remembered. She didn't remember his face, nor would she ever... but she would never forget the kind hands of a protecting father.

Rissling watched them head to Josef and Klaus's barracks. He would keep a close eye on them. There was nothing in their paperwork but accolades and recommendations, but Rissling knew all it took was a word from him to change all that. He would bide his time. The child would be his again to command.

Rissling smiled the feral smile of a predator ready to pounce on his prey. Rissling would get her again. He could wait. After all, hunters were nothing, if not very patient waiting for the perfect moment to attack. Yes, he was a top predator. He flexed his arms inside his jacket sleeves. He might not be as rock hard and lean as Klaus and Josef, but they were weak. He was in his prime. He was nearly perfect. They were flawed.

The villagers had assembled once more in the blacksmith shop. With much talking in the last week, they had come up with a plan. They had enlisted the help of a young adult, Dorek. With everyone slowly working together, silently under the cover of darkness, and countless yards of black fabric to hide them, they had managed to make a small hole underneath the fence at the farthest point at the camp away from the village.

The brave young Dorek had gladly offered to assist and had been using the smallest of hand shovels over the course of the last week to dig the hole. Once he had gotten through to the other side, another younger child had joined him and they had placed a dirty rag over the top of the hole, being careful to avoid the razor wire and electrified wires. The rag was stretched over the hole and strategically placed rocks held it in place. Carefully they had tossed handfuls of dirt over the rag to hopefully disguise it from a casual observer.

Tonight they would sneak into the camp and pull out a couple of prisoners if they could. The ever irritating, Antone Lienschoff was still yelling to whoever would listen to him in the jail house about the terrible rule breaking going on.

As the moon crept slowly to the other side of the world, the small group of men and women reached the fence. As they had hoped, a few people had heard about the escape plan and some of the more able bodied had assembled. It wasn't hard to keep quiet. Every calorie they had was used just to get to the wall. There wasn't any left over for socializing. The quiet group waited with two of their members facing the inside of the camp to watch for any approaching guards.

"Don't move until we tell you, and then when you do push the smallest ones through first. We have to get the fence ready, so wait...and for god's sake...and all of ours, please don't make any noise." The gruff whisper of the blacksmith sounded in the hollow yard. His beard lay in the dirt and his eyes met those of a prisoner on the other side. The prisoner nodded and laid his head in the dirt and closed his eyes. Just a brief rest before his poor body needed to work again.

On the far side of the jail wall back in the village, the woman stood; a dark scarf covering her face. Tendrils of her sandy blond hair with all its grey escaped her scarf and waved softly in the breeze. Antone was her friend, and she believed he was right. Helping those Jewish pigs was just asking for trouble. It would endanger their entire village! Those stupid do-gooders in her village would bring the entire wrath of the Nazi Regime upon them. Didn't they know she had a son to protect?

They didn't seem much like mother and son, but she loved him and would do nearly anything to protect him, especially if that meant bringing attention to her.

She would speak to Antone this night and then march right up to the gate with her information! Besides asking for help to keep the angry blacksmith and his loudmouth away from her, she planned to tell every guard she could about these awful villagers who would threaten her life with their idiotic planning.

Susi Wyesein was no shirking coward. She knew what she would tell the guards. All she had to do was visit her friend and find out where the escape would happen and when. She didn't know that the villagers had been careful to conceal all information from Antone. She never thought to wonder why she didn't know anything either. Antone and Susi were of the same cloth.

Turning from friend to enemy in an instant was a common theme with both of them. Being overly friendly one moment, long enough to gain information...and the next just walking away and giving whatever information, no matter how miniscule to pretty much the highest bidder. Whatever would make them seem as though they were more important than the others. Whatever would make them both appear more than what they were was their asking price.

A hushed whisper toward the barred window had Antoine sitting up quickly and rubbing his eyes. He thought he had heard a noise, but wasn't sure. He slowly walked to the window to carefully peer out.

He knew the villagers had spoken of him, and not with admiration, but with disdain. He knew if from the children running past and throwing rocks in his window. "Dorftrottel!" became a local children's cry as they passed the jail laughing at him.

He was not the village idiot. He was damn far from it! He was simply a villager in a field full of nothing but idiots! He would show them. Somehow, he would get back at them for the ridicule they had bestowed upon him.

Quietly in the dark of night, Antone and Susi began to figure out a plan as to how to save their village from the danger, not to mention felonious activities many of their villagers were bringing upon their village. These people needed to be stopped.

Susi handed in a pie she had made. It would help bolster her friend's spirits. How dare they incarcerate him for speaking the truth and talking from his heart. Didn't they know he was right? To try to save someone no one even cared about and endanger their own people was wrong.

She smiled as she turned away from the jail wall. They had a plan to stop these idiots who would have them all killed.

Chapter 12

Hanna hadn't gone that next day, but during the next week. Hanna was ready. Eva was still so very sore, but they had to get out. Rissling was always watching for Eva. Every morning, Eva was sent to work at the new Commander's barracks alone. She seemed to be healthier than she was before. She almost seemed to have a little more than just skin stretched over her bones. Hanna sighed, knowing it was nothing more than her own hope tricking her eyes into believing her child was looking better every day.

Then one day, Rissling showed up earlier than Klaus or Josef. He yanked Eva out of the bunk and brought her to his barracks. He again beat Eva that day; yesterday.

Today she would leave. They might die trying, but Hanna was getting her baby out of here. She had to. Her daughter could not die at the hands of that monster; of any of these monsters.

Hanna crept to the fence. She had meant to escape right then and there when she returned to her barracks, but her poor, bruised Eva had suffered so much that day and was sleeping. While Hanna had finished the dinner for the Camp Commander, Eva had been tucked into her barrack bunk by Marta and held close as she slept.

Hanna too had slept and it was already late. The grey light of dawn was already beginning to show. Eva was already stiff and sore and was unusually, though rightfully so, grumpy and not listening.

Hanna had noticed several times where small holes had been being dug under the hold fence and rags were stuffed in them to conceal the holes. Today she would push Eva and maybe herself beneath the wire and take their chances outside of this hell.

"Quickly Eva, I know you hurt but you need to move now" Hanna hissed as she tried to push her daughter beneath the first fence.

Eva pushed herself along, whimpering in pain. "No Momma." Eva lay still in the dirt. Hanna sobbed; this had all been so very simple as she had been planning her escape. Actually implementing it was a far different deal.
Hanna barely heard the clink of the clip on the rifle sling as it hit the barrel of the rifle.
"Stoppen!" The single word felt as though it had twisted a knife deep in her heart. What's worse, she recognized the voice. None other than Klaus Strochmoer, the new camp commander.

Klaus had his rifle trained at Hanna's face. She looked up at him, some of her hair covering her eyes. Eva whimpered once more and began to push her way back into the fence Hanna had so desperately tried to push her out of. Her Eva was trying to crawl *toward* Klaus!

At the sound of running feet Hanna looked over her shoulder and then softly laid her head on the ground. She was done. She and Eva would die this day. The sobs so long pushed back into her soul came forward. She cried. She cried for her small child, so innocent. For the millions of others just like her that knew what they were facing, without any possibility of escape.

Without bothering to wipe to wipe her eyes or her face she slowly pushed herself off the ground and pulled her child into her arms. At least she would die facing her killers; facing all the monsters head on.

She stood as tall as she could. Hoping she could at least pretend she was not trembling and crying inside.

Klaus too, had seen Eva reach for him before he looked behind him and saw Rissling running to the scene with several other guards- Josef in the lead. He sighed in relief when Josef met his eyes. Several times, Eva had come to their barracks under Josef's watchful eye. Eva was somewhat of a regular 'visitor' to their kitchen. Always, she stayed in 'her' spot. They had even placed a cushion covered crate for her to sit or lay on. She was almost like a pet, Klaus told himself. You get attached to them, even if they were strays. Klaus had watched Rissling many a time as Josef walked Eva to their barracks.

Both men knew Rissling seemed to be staring at her more often with a predatory glaze. Perhaps it was the fact that Eva had been in the company of Josef and Klaus that it spurred some kind of jealous *thing* within him. His animosity toward the young girl had grown exponentially, the longer that she was in the company of Josef and Klaus. Watching Rissling come stalking closer to the child Klaus felt the hair on the back of his neck stand up.

Rissling's eyes seemed almost glazed over and were focused on the child. From the corner of his mouth, a small bit of drool edged out. The man was planning terrible things ahead for this innocent kid.

Klaus, for his credit did not sit with that kind of child abuse. It seemed out of odds with a man who seemed perfectly ok with killing children; he just didn't want them hurt first-and not like that. He couldn't stand how much Eva, every day, reminded him more of the young sister he had loved with everything a boy could possess. Klaus narrowed his eyes at Rissling knowing and almost feeling the excitement emanating from the man.

Josef reached Klaus's side first and met his friend's eyes again. Rissling was fast approaching and his eyes seemed to sparkle with glee. He had a spring that could only mean a terrible death sentence for Eva, unless Josef and Klaus could think of something quickly to spare her such an awful death sentence. Something that wouldn't let anyone else know they were actively trying to save the child.

"So you were going to sneak out of here?" Rissling stepped forward and reached for Eva. "I'm going to enjoy teaching her a few lessons about why you don't run." He laughed the sound seeming to echo in her head. "She won't be able to run at all when I am finished with her," Rissling sneered again.

Rissling grabbed Eva's fore arm and began to drag her toward him with an ugly sneer on his face. Hanna seemed frozen until Eva's shrill scream broke through the soft morning mist. Hanna jumped at the sound and pulled her daughter towards her and spat in Rissling's face.

Rissling stood for a moment, almost confused. No one had ever dared to demean him like that, especially a whore! As he began to reach for his pistol Klaus spoke, loud enough for all assembled to hear. His tone brooked no argument. "Hanna, you will regret that decision for the rest of your life. You never threaten an officer." He looked to the officers amassed. "Josef take her child to the crematory and kill her."

Josef saw Rissling open his mouth to defy the order, and nodded quickly. Josef didn't want to kill the child, but Klaus was right. A quick death was far more humane than a death the type Rissling seemed to have planned. Before Rissling could actually speak, Josef walked to cut in front of Rissling and wrenched the small girl from her mother.

Hanna wouldn't let go of her child and Josef grabbed her. His fingers were like iron bars as he pressed the space between the ligaments in her wrist. Pain shot through her arm, as the surprised look befell her face. Her baby was going to die and she caused it. Her arm ceased to work from the pain and her fingers slowly left her baby. She knew it would be the last time she ever felt her child again. It was all her fault.

Josef gathered the child in his arms roughly and strode away. Hanna's wail echoed in his ears. Just as Hanna made to jump onto Josef's back Klaus grabbed her wrenched her to his chest. Her arms were caught in an impossible vice and her back was getting jabbed by whatever he had on his shirt.

Hanna screamed again, "Eva! Oh God! Evaaaa!!! Oh baby, my beautiful baby. You can't take her. Take me instead. Oh God! Take me instead, take me with her!"

Hanna slowly sank to her knees and Klaus let her fall heavily to the hard ground. Rissling turned with a sneer to Hanna, "I'm going to help her die, for your sins."

The leer as he turned his head was not lost on Heinrich and Jonah's. Both men glanced at each other, knowing the small child would not die well if Rissling was involved. Several of the male and a couple of the female officers turned to follow Rissling. Depravity knew know bounds.

Of the many assembled guards, two met eyes and turned to face Klaus. The older guard Heinrich, and his constant companion, the young Jonah watched as the group of "soldiers" followed Josef. Heinrich watched the clenched jaw move on Klaus's face and knew that Klaus knew as well as he did, what Rissling and the other soldiers had planned for the small girl.

"Klaus!" Heinrich shouted, "Let's have Josef bring the girl back her to bury her where her mom can see it. We'll wait here, and watch her. She can dig the grave right here. "

Rissling stopped and turned his mouth hanging open. What treasonous action was this? Now that damn Heinrich with the ugly mustache and his stupid kid companion were thwarting him too?

A couple of the other guards groaned and began walking off in different directions. Only a couple stayed to watch the mother Jew see her dead child; some were whispering excitedly among themselves. Men and women alike, some would stay to watch the show.

Chapter 13

Eva chose that moment to become aware of what was happening and went to scream. Josef quickly clamped his hand over her mouth to keep her silent. A quick death was far better than a slow one that Rissling would have her endure. He held her silent against him until he got around to the crematory.

Several prisoners were already in attendance working. Josef noticed one looked at him, directly at him while the others pretended not to see him. He saw it was the same older man he had met on the tour; the old man that seemed to peer into his very soul.

The man sent the two other workers scurrying away with a wave of his hand to collect the dead. They would collect the bodies that the cold night and meager food rations had accumulated. They slowly trod to the dirt path on their usual morning walk. The walk that they would one day not have to do; someone else would be doing the same walk and would be bringing them in to the ever hungry flames of the ovens.

When the two weary prisoners left the crematory the old man walked to Josef. He looked down at the girl and shook his head. Eva was a beautiful child. So terrible it was that she must die. That all the children would die.

Josef wasn't sure how the man knew he was here to kill the child, but looking at him, he almost felt the sorrow coming from the old man. The sorrow of a man that thought he had seen it all and then more just kept right on coming at him, now in the form of a small child about to meet her fate.

The old man walked over to give one last blessing to the child. Surely this man, even an SS, would see that. As the man bent to the child, the young one reached out her hand without hesitation or fear.

"What happened, Grandfather?" The child put her hand to the old man's face. He had been pulling another load of bodies when he had fallen and slipped several days before. Inside the squalid conditions of the camp the wound quickly became infected and inflamed. The area around his eye was sloughing off. He knew only by feel how bad it must look. The old man knew his time here was short. At least one of the last things he could do in his life would be to bless this poor child's soul, before the sickness and fever took his life from him. Josef watched as the old man bent closer to the child. He pulled her small hand away from his infected wound. "It is nothing child, only but a scratch, nothing for you to worry about."

Eva looked up at Josef through her bruised face and the one eye with blood pooled in it. "Will he be ok Josef?" Josef looked down at this small ragged scrap of humanity. She had heard every word. She may be bruised but he knew those small ears worked just fine. He met the old man's eyes. "Yes. She knows. She worries too much about others." The man looked down and touched the girl's bruised face, "She would even forgive the one who has done this."

Josef looked around at the sickening site. He had to kill the girl, to walk back and hand her to Rissling was not an option. She would die quickly, by his own hand as painlessly as he could make it. It was the only thing, the only mercy he could offer her.

He had wasted too much time already, but could do one more thing for the child. One small kindness before her world was no more. He bent to the child, after looking quickly around for any wandering eyes. He pulled the small child to him and embraced her gently. He could do this. One small kindness in such a hell she had found herself in, through no fault of her own; through the fault of men like him who were too cowardly to stand up against evil.

Josef hugged the child and pulled out his pistol. "It's ok. I am tired, Josef.

Momma said I would go to a big sleep if we were caught-ed" The old man, inhaled with a catch in his throat and stood to turn away. He could not bear to look. Pulling even the smallest bodies from the barracks was one thing. Watching another single child be murdered in cold blood was another.

The old man's back was to Josef and gave him enough pause to look around, witness to the deaths of innocents. Bodies of all sorts lay strewn around him. Josef looked with almost new eyes. When the Old man realized that Josef had not yet shot, he chanced a look behind him. Josef's eyes were no longer on the young child; they were looking near the old man at the ground. A child lay motionless on the ground. The skin on the child still fresh, not covered in soot, dirt and vermin like so many of the others.

The old man turned and stared once more in Josef's soul. He pointed to the dead child. "The child was just sent on by his mother only minutes ago. She couldn't bear to see the child suffer any more." The old man paused, "The child is male, but is the same size."

He looked down at Eva and smiled a gentle, grandfatherly smile. He bent to pick up an adult shirt from the ground and gave it a shake. "Give me your dress, quickly child" Eva nodded and pulled the dress over her small frame with its ribs and shoulder blades sticking out obscenely, the bruises still glaring madly from her thin skin. The old man tossed the adult shirt to Josef and turned to the child's body on the ground.

"Here." Eva obediently handed the dress to the old man. He patted her head gently and nodded to Josef.

As though he were under a spell Josef found himself pulling the adult size shirt over young Eva's shoulders until her head popped out through the top. She nearly giggled as she held out her arms, the sleeves dangling off the ends of her arms. "Child quickly, there is a spot no one will check inside the other oven room. It is not working behind that wall, hide there. Someone will get you. Say not a word child. Let no one see you! God be with you."

Eva scrambled away, running quickly to the spot directed. The old man held the body of the child. "A life for a life, we will spare the child Josef."
Josef held the old man's gaze and pulled the trigger.

He had watched, almost the casual observer as the old man held the dead child close and pointed at his own throat. His throat would kill him, though not as quickly, but would ensure a bloody body to bring back. Josef knew the old man was close to death. The pallor of his fever evident on his aged face, the man blinked slowly and pulled the dead child tighter to his chest. He met Josef's eyes and nodded.

As Josef fired the shot into the exposed jugular of the old man, he watched as the blood started slowly trickling and then pulsing out of the wound to cover the young child. The old man slowly sank to the ground, as though he was being helped by the hand of God, and maybe he was. He softly sat with the child.

Josef walked to the old man. With the last bit of life in his body, the old man smiled at Josef and then fell backward to the ground. Josef looked down at the lifeless bodies and sighed. He had done the old man a mercy, he knew that…yet it still hurt his heart. Eva was alive though; however, he didn't know how long she would stay that way.

He gathered the blood stained body of the child to him, careful to not show the identity of the child. Fortunately, the child's hair was close to the same color. He could only hope that Hanna, in her grief did not notice the differences in the children. If anyone of the prisoners noticed that the child's body was not Eva's, they didn't seem to care.

Hanna couldn't pull herself up off of the ground. Heaving with heavy sobs as she mentally calculated the steps it was going to take Josef to bring her child to the crematory and kill her.

After what seemed like forever, that dreaded single gunshot echoed across the field. Her life would never be the same, she might as well be dead instead. Maybe she already was. At the sound she wailed once more. "Evaaaaaa!!!!!" and collapsed into the ground.

Rissling couldn't let a good opportunity go. "Hear that? Hear that sound? A bullet hits a body at that range, even a child's body, you can hear the difference." He laughed as he looked down at the woman near his feet. He kicked dirt into her face and spit on her exposed arm. He turned to watch Josef return with the dead child.

Hanna continued to cry, looking up once to see her child's limp body strewn over his arm. Blood dripped down his uniform sleeve from her child's body. A small, barely visible mist of red was on his shoulders and neck. She watched the blood drip from his sleeve where he held her child as it hit the dirt in front of him. "Oh God...no. What have you done?" Hanna screamed once more. Klaus pointed to the shallow grave recently dug. Josef turned on his heel and tossed the body in. The sickening almost liquid thud as her child's body hit the ground was a sound that she would never forget. Her life was over. Eva's blood stained dress was clearly visible as the prisoners Jonah ordered over began to bury the small body. One of their own, their youngest.

Hanna would never remember how she had gotten back to her barracks but it would be hours until she became aware enough to realize she was in her own bunk and Marta was holding her tightly. Hanna cried over and over throughout the night until finally exhaustion over took her and she slept.

Chapter 14

Rissling was annoyed. Once more the illustrious Klaus and Josef had purposely thwarted him.

To sport with the child was not something he had ever done before. It wasn't something he had entertained, he wasn't interested in it, but his latest Jew play toys were not as much as they used to be. Several days earlier when he had been flinging the young Eva around, he had been surprised to feel a stirring. It was much like the feeling he got when he forced a young man to submit to his cravings.

He felt sure that no one could notice what his intentions had been for the child, not even realizing that he had made the threat out loud. It seemed everyone had known what his plans were.

He would deal with Klaus and Josef in his own time. For now though, he would wait. He would bide his time. He only had a while longer in this stinking cesspool and then he was gone. He had received his papers but the thrill of the camp, without the hassle of running it excited him as it had no other time.

With the morning excitement over the men walked away. Some of the men complaining that they didn't get to watch Rissling take care of the child and that they didn't get to watch the young Jew pig watch her child die. A few wondered why they hadn't taken care of the child in front of the mother. Now that would have been a fitting punishment!

Josef and Klaus walked back to the barracks. It was over. Klaus couldn't help but feel utterly helpless in that situation. It was a feeling he rarely ever got. He was pissed. He didn't necessarily mind giving a kill order, or even seem to care about the mother's cries, beside the fact that they were annoying.

He didn't care much about Josef and his bleeding heart, knowing that if given a choice, the child would rather die quickly than at the hands of that kind of torment. As far as he was concerned, the kill order was a mercy.

He figured he would almost kind of miss that cute stray following him around inside his barracks when she was there. Not that he had liked her at all, but like any kind of stray creature, you simply just got used to it being there.

He was a bit glad though that she was gone, selfishly, if only to not keep making him feel so protective of her, as he had been with his little sister so long ago.

He might, had he let himself feel, discover that he actually was a very small bit fond of the child. She was so innocent and yet so fearless. So obviously terrified, but yet incredibly brave that young stray kid had been. He might have even gone so far as to think he might have actually respected the little shit if she had been the right race.

What annoyed him though, was the commander. Seeing the glint in his eyes and according to talk among the men, Rissling had something terrible planned for the child. That in and of its self wasn't the problem. That a child would die at the hands of his countrymen wasn't actually such a big deal. It happened every day.

How it would have been done actually did bother him though. Kill the vermin, that was fine…but there was no reason to assault a child in that manner; that kind of manner was just wrong. Extermination was one thing. One might have to do that from time to time. Reveling in debauchery was a different kettle of fish. It was pure disgusting. One didn't even joke about that kind of thing.

What bothered Klaus the most, was the fact that he had been forced to make decisions that he didn't feel like making. He hated feeling forced to make decisions on someone else's time frame. That damn Rissling. Had he not come skulking around like a feral dog, things might have gone quite differently for the child.

As the men continued walking, Klaus looked over to his good friend Josef. He noticed Josef was quite quiet, yet the fact that he had just walked over and killed the child he had actually liked didn't seem to bother him. Klaus furrowed his brow. He was wondering what had actually happened or if Josef was having a bit of a mental break. It was known to happen to many officers. The stress and burden of such a horrific, yet necessary, 'job' was often more than many could stomach for long.

Josef looked almost lost in thought. It was a face Klaus knew well. Josef wasn't suffering a mental lapse. He was up to something. Klaus also knew his stubborn friend wouldn't say a single word until he felt like it.

Klaus turned his eyes from Josef and looked to their barracks. He smiled. His friend was stubborn, but he could out stubborn him every time. With that decided, Klaus turned his thoughts on what to get for breakfast.

Josef's thoughts weren't exactly far from Klaus's own, with the exception of one small detail, which was presently hiding behind the non-functional oven in a shirt six sizes too big.

He hadn't had much time to think through his actions earlier. The old man hadn't helped much by suggesting he save the child. Now that he had, he found he didn't know what to do. What the hell does one do as an SS guard, with a Jewish girl child to hide in a god damned concentration camp?

Josef looked down at his blood stained uniform. He remembered again how the old man so willingly gave his life for that of the child. He was obviously going to be dying soon, but with his last breath he ensured at least one child of the next generation would live. At least that day... that one day... the future would live. His story, all their stories would be told. The old man ensured the future, he had paid for that future with his life.

Josef strode into the barracks removing his jacket as he went. He tossed it into the hamper and began to unbutton his shirt. On the third button down, he heard Klaus's lighter and sharp inhale of breath. He looked up to meet Klaus's quizzical gaze.

"You ass, I know you are up to something. I just don't know what yet."

Josef returned to his buttons and pulled off his shirt. His white undershirt rode tightly on chest and arms. He threw the shirt onto the hamper; blood from the sleeve hitting the wall behind and leaving a smear. It glared at him, evidence of the last bit of life from an old man who gave all to save the life of one tiny, fortunate girl.

Klaus inhaled deeply on his cigarette, turning his head slightly from the smoke curling up towards his eyes. He watched as Josef sat quiet for a moment and then turned to the table. Josef poured some whiskey into a glass and downed it.

Klaus followed and grabbed the bottle from Josef, the cigarette between his lips as he poured from the bottle into his glass. Klaus's gaze went from the blood stained wall and back to his friend as he set the bottle down and grabbed the cigarette from his lips. He downed the shot as he looked once more at the bloodstain on the wall.

He sputtered, "God dammit Josef!" He set his glass hard down on the table and turned to face his old friend. "She's still alive isn't she?"

Josef could only nod. He wasn't sure how he could explain it to Klaus; he barely could explain it to himself. He hardly understood how it had happened. He wasn't sure there even was an explanation. To say it seemed as though the old man had put him under a spell was sure to sound even worse than a simple "I changed my mind" would have been.

Josef had saved a child, but in doing so had signed their own death sentences should the child...no *when* the child was found. There was no way an officer could hide a child from a thousand prying eyes.

Chapter 15

Eva hid behind the ovens as she had been told to do by the old man. In her exhausted state and being fairly warm near the oven's heat she fell asleep. She was near so many dead bodies, but after living with the dead and the walking dead for the last few months of her life, scenes like this were barely unusual anymore. She still made sure not to touch any bodies, but she wasn't overly afraid.

The old man told her to hide and she would. She didn't know what she would do if no one came for her, but she didn't worry over much about it. The adults in her life, Momma and Marta, always told her the truth, even if they didn't like to do it. They always did what they said. Eva had no reason to worry this would be anything different. She had no way to know that Josef had saved her from a fate worse than death, until finally death would come to hold her hand. She had no knowledge of what the personal cost it would be to him.

Years later, if she survived that long, she would look back on this day and realize what Josef had actually done for her and to him. She had no way of knowing that his decision could cost his life.

Eva curled up in the farthest darkest corner and wrapped the shirt tightly around her. She was used to hearing the noise, the talking and the smells. The litters dragging along the broken ground carrying the dead were a common noise and the girl slept through all of them. She would never know the old man's sacrifice, or how he had gone in her stead. She had already hid when he willingly gave his life for her. She slept on, knowing and trusting the only adults in her life that she was close to. She was told they would come for her, so they would. She slept a deep healing sleep in the corner of the oven room.

The body of the old man would vanish. Only one witness to the kindness had seen what had happened. A young Jewish man named Jules had been one of the workers. While the old man had been near the child and Josef, he had lifted his hand in Jules directions, letting the young man know to duck and stay out of sight. He had, and then he had witnessed the old man's sacrifice and the act of kindness from the SS officer. When Eva had run away to hide, and the old man had fallen, Jules had carefully picked up the old man's shovel and carried it away from the crematory to set it where the old man usually sat.

Then he had run back into the alleyway and quickly pulled the man to the ovens. With what he thought had to be super human strength he had been able to throw the old man into the oven. The evidence of the German officers 'treachery' would never be known. One single burned skull would never be investigated. There were millions of those in this hell around him. The old man lying dead when others returned, with a bullet torn throat would however be looked into, and Jules couldn't let the old man's sacrifice be in vain.

After he had attended to the body, Jules ran back to his barracks, lest anyone suspect him of being a witness. He ran back to his younger brother Sam and his brother's friend Jared and curled into the bunk next to them. It had been sad to see the old man die. It was a turning of a page, an ending. The old man had though, chosen his own path. His death was his way out of hell. His death would stand as testament to the value of a life- of all life. He had died so that another would live. He died an old man to allow the future of his world to live on. The SS officer had accepted his terms and a girl remained alive and unharmed. For now.

Jules pretended to go back to sleep. The guards would be out soon to oversee the tasks of the prisoners. He had not been on the dead clean up; he had only ventured out to see what the fuss was about. He had seen the commotion near the fence and had watched as the SS carried the child. At first he had wanted to throw a portion of the brick into the man's skull when he had seen Josef's hand over Eva's mouth, but then he had noticed the man was stopping the child from screaming to protect her, not to brutalize her.

At the scene he had had to shake his head to make sure he wasn't seeing things when he watched the guard kneel and take the child into his arms. He alone knew the secret. He was a marked man if anyone else had seen him. Many of his fellow Jews had turned on each other. Running to the guards for any infraction, no matter how slight, in the hopes that a slight garnered favor might be bought. It wasn't always, but it was enough for there to be a hope that some special favor might come their way.

It wasn't that the Germans wanted to give favors, of course it wasn't. Monsters didn't give favors. Of that, in this time, everyone was sure. The old man had told him in one of their many clandestine talks that it was simply another form of control. To divide the prisoners, to make it be their fault they were working separately from each other was better for the Germans. It was a common theme, a simple theme. Divide and then conquer.

The Germans had little to no fear of an uprising by the prisoner population. Any talk of one could be overheard and reported. Sometimes the smallest infractions were reported. An extra dipper of water here, two crusts of bread there...it all made sense to the old man. Try as he might, he could never convince the prisoners to believe him. Someone always talked.

An extra meal, an extra favor, and even the removal of a soul that one simply didn't like could sometimes occur for bringing in information...and that hope kept the information coming to the German soldiers like clockwork.

Sometimes the informants just disappeared. Prisoners would believe that the informant had been set free. They never were. The old man had seen enough to know they were only set free via the chimney smoke. It was hit or miss, telling the Germans. You might get a reward, you probably wouldn't. It was a gamble. It was a simple, yet complex roulette game of life. It was either hope and promise, or death. But it was enough, just enough hope to keep it repeating over and over again. Many a nation had been felled by just such a strategy.

The old man had quietly talked to the young Jules over the course of the time they had known each other. The old man had probably saved his life, and that of his brother many times. "Talk to no one. Say nothing to no one. Trust only in me and in yourself. In here your life could be worth no more than a crust of bread or an extra turnip, or it could be worth nothing" ...and it usually was.

Because of those talks, Jules had mastered the art of playing his luck. He observed the officers, just enough to start to follow their routines. However it may have appeared, the camp was actually quite methodic and ritualized. It was this ritual that helped Jules keep himself, his younger brother Sam and his brother's young friend alive.

It was the old man who had taught him to keep his mouth shut and his eyes open. It was this concentration on living and being aware that helped them all. Well, that and a hell of a lot of sheer luck.

Jules heard the roll call and bade Sam a good bye. He would stand for hours this day. His hopes had been buoyed by the scene he had witnessed. It gave him hope; real hope that he and his brother might live.

Chapter 16

"God damn Josef!" Klaus pounded the table with both his hands. "Damn it Josef!"

Klaus threw his cigarette at Josef's face and stalked out the door. Josef poured another drink for himself and downed that one too. There was nothing left for him here. He had made a decision that could kill his best friend, not to mention himself...and Hanna and Eva when Eva was discovered.

What was done was done. He couldn't change the fact that the child was still very much alive now. He could go back and kill her, but now there would be too many witnesses to see her alive and know. He could only hope that the child would be found by someone other than Rissling or that somehow, something good would come of this. He didn't see how anything could, of course...but what was done was done. There was nothing left to do, but face the consequences of his actions.

He sighed as he slowly walked to his bunk and grabbed his bag. Instead of just haphazardly throwing stuff into his bag and walking away, he realized that to save his friend, he would have to leave slowly lest he pique the wrong person's interest. Klaus could not be killed for *his* 'crime'. He had to protect his friend. He wasn't worried about himself but Klaus, that damned arrogant bastard, could not die for Josef's sins. He wouldn't allow it. Klaus was his brother. He loved him. It was that simple. He would leave so his brother would live.

Meticulously, he began to pack his belongings in his bags. He would think of some kind of an acceptable excuse and leave whatever he couldn't take with Klaus. His mind made up, Josef packed and formulated his story. He wondered briefly if he could stow the child in his pack. If she so much as made a peep though, he would be killed on the spot and Rissling would get exactly what he wanted.

It would be hours and nearly dark until Klaus returned. Josef had packed and then gone on to supervise the next 'dig site' or mass grave. Klaus walked in and looked at the neatly packed bags on Josef's bed.

"That horse's ass!" Klaus stood looking a few minutes longer. He knew Josef's heart as he knew his own. Josef was going to leave, to take all the blame when the child was found alive. He knew that Josef knew that he would be killed for his traitorous ways.

Klaus checked his watch. Josef would be back in an hour, possibly a few minutes more. He also knew that damn fool would have some kind of a story made up. "Stupid fool probably stood here, feeling sorry for himself and concocting up some bullshit story."

It was in fact; exactly what Josef had done earlier that day.

Klaus shook his head as he walked into the kitchen. It would be some ridiculous bleeding heart story about how he was sorry and he must leave in order for Klaus to live. Some martyred up story for the other officers about a sick grandmother or some other horse shit tale. That damn pansy ass bleeding heart, Josef!

Klaus stood at the table, both hands flat on the table top and his head hanging down looking at the floor. With his one leg straight and the other one at ease, he looked calm were anyone to see him. Inside though, he was angrier than he could ever remember being at his friend. Josef hadn't even given him a chance to be a friend, to help him. That jackass just assumed he would be mad and... Klaus shook his head. Of course he would! And of course he was pissed! But that didn't mean that *Josef the great* shouldn't have given him a chance to get pissed off at him!

How dare that ass just walk out and leave him here alone! It wasn't like he couldn't handle it, he could... and probably easier without some pansy like Josef turning sad eyes on every Jew he saw. Klaus knew he was being unreasonable towards his friend, but he was pissed. Josef had taken Klaus's CHOICE to be pissed off! Klaus grabbed his hat off the rack and slammed it on his head. He stalked out the door for the second time in one day because of Josef.

The light was just about the same grey as it had been this morning when Eva and Hanna had been caught trying to escape. The light was fading fast now though, instead of this morning with the new dawn coming in. Klaus strode straight towards the ovens. It was the last place the girl had been, so she must still be somewhere over there. As dumb as Josef could be at times, even he wouldn't have been dumb enough to do anything with the child where someone could see him. He hoped anyway.

Klaus stood near the end of the Officers barracks, closest the crematory. Roll call would sound in just a few minutes or so and Rissling was in charge. That meant Klaus would have, if Rissling was his usual, several hours in which to find the child.

His friend might hate him, it could sever their childhood bond...hell it would sever their friendship, but the child would die today. He couldn't let his friend take the fall and possibly die for a child that was nothing to him.

There was no way in hell that Josef was taking off and then that damn kid was going to come slinking around and leave Klaus standing there holding the proverbial bag. Rissling would crow to anyone and everyone about Josef's treason. Klaus was damn sure not going to bat for some Jewish rat-ling.

As the roll call horn sounded, Klaus strode from behind the buildings as though he were out on detail. He was, but it was his own detail. He would finish the job that Josef failed to do. Assuring the death of the child would spare Josef and his own life. He had to kill the child, and he had to do it now before she was found by anyone else. As the last of the prisoners shuffled off for the yard, Klaus walked slowly through the crematory. He had to kill the child with Sonja's eyes, before she got them all killed.

Bodies lay stacked, most of them naked, thin limbs almost intertwined. Klaus rarely walked the crematorium and felt a slight stirring of pity standing there alone among the dead. He didn't put it into so many words, but it was the first of that feeling he had ever had. God damn Josef was contagious.

He walked a few more feet and looked closely at the stacked bodies, looking for anything that resembled a still living child. With roll call currently happening, Klaus realized the crematory was deathly quiet with the exception of the slight hissing and crackling from the ovens. He almost felt eyes on him as he searched for the child. It was an uncomfortable feeling and Klaus didn't like it. He got even angrier at Josef. "Damn foolish man, always crying over something!" He muttered as he continued his search for the one small gem in the deepest bowels of hell.

As the minutes stretched on he found himself feeling as though the hair on the back of his neck was starting to rise. It didn't help that it was nearly dark out now. He could see the fields and the tree line in the distance, but looking at the dark recesses of the building stacked with the dead it was nearly impossible to see.

An occasional glint of a buckle or button, not yet removed from the dead would catch his glance, looking as though an accusing eye were glaring at him. Klaus stood a moment longer and turned in the center of the yard. Pale limbs of the dead almost seemed to glow as the moon continued its rise. Their sunken, almost black eye sockets and mouths stared at him, looking as though they could come back to life any second…if only to kill him for interrupting their nightmares.

Chapter 17

He turned quickly on his heel to leave when he felt a presence. He spun quickly around, his eyes darting back and forth as the searched for whatever was out there stalking him. At the light touch on his back he spun again drawing his pistol and holding it out in front of him. He turned slowly, in a full circle, seeing nothing but the pale corpses. He slowly holstered his Walther p38, not bothering to close the flap on it. His hand shook slightly as he released his pistol. He was getting out of here. He would come back at first light and find her and dispatch of her then. He wasn't scared of course, he simply didn't like it here and there was no way he was going to find a dumb kid in the dark anyway.

With his decision made, he began to relax, trying to stifle a yawn after holding his breath so long. When he felt a light, but ice cold touch on his hand, it felt like a dead child's hand. Working for these months in the camp he had felt the ice cold flesh of the dead many times. The cold, yet very small hand gripped again, slightly harder this time.

Klaus recoiled his hand at the same time his body involuntarily tried to finish his yawn. He tried to yell, even though his yawn had not quite finished. The sound of his yelling as his body finished the yawn came out as a combination of the two, a terrible combination of the two.

The squeak that came out of his mouth was utterly embarrassing. He heard a thud and felt the ground vibrate near his feet. He jumped, trying to run in different directions from this spirit filled place. Both feet moving at once, while his brain tried to catch up had him looking as though he were dancing a jig while squeaking of all things, like a god damned idiot.

He looked down at the sound of a small giggle. He looked to see a cherubic face looking up and him and giggling. The sound was as out of place as a church choir would have been in this dark alley surrounded by the dead.

Klaus readied himself to reach down and yank the child to her feet. How dare she laugh at him? As he began to reach, another quiet giggle stopped him in his tracks. The sound was a sweet, soft bell in the bowels of hell. The same giggle Sonja had when she was so young, and he a small boy himself.

Not knowing exactly what to do in this terribly embarrassing and odd situation, Klaus put his hands on hips and scowled down. His scowl normally sent prisoners and fellow officers running away, usually in fear. The small giggle raised slightly in volume. "Kraus! You squeaked like the mouse's do!"

Eva put both of her stained and grubby hands to her mouth to stifle the next round of giggles. "That's why you said you didn't like me and called me a kitty cat!" She looked up at him again, her oversize shirt with both her thin, emaciated shoulders nearly popping out the top. "It's because you squeak like a mouse!"

Something akin to humor settled in Klaus's chest. He wanted to laugh, but no one dared, even the youngest of Jew pigs, to laugh at a Waffen-SS! He hadn't laughed in a while and the feeling kept coming up at him. He was a man torn. He had come to both find the child and kill her himself, or better yet bring her back to Josef to finish the job with his bare hands. He deserved that for putting his very own life at risk for a Jew rat. He found himself instead staring down into a slight, bruised face and listening to a small girl giggle innocently at him and wanting to chuckle along with her.

It had to be just the eerie silence and almost paranormal experience of earlier that had him so flummoxed. He came here to kill the little shit and damned if he wasn't standing there among the corpses feeling that damn laugh coming on.

He looked away from the child and back toward the main yard. A tiny voice from at his feet went "squeak!" He looked down into her smiling face with the tiny white teeth shining in the dark and laughed. He closed his eyes and laughed, the laughter taking him by surprise. It took only that single split second of laughter, but he made his decision. He would bring the child back to Josef to kill. He wasn't weak, and sure he could kill this child as easily as he wanted too, but he would leave it to Josef instead. It was all his doing; he started it...so he could finish it. Klaus would leave it for Josef to do.

Klaus knelt down. "I go on my round soon. I will get you then. You will follow me, but in the dark far behind me. You got that?"

Eva tried to stand, still a bit awkward with her sore body and ended up with her long sleeves getting stuck beneath her feet, threatening to trip her and topple over on her face. "Oh for Christs sake!" Klaus grabbed her roughly by the upper arms and stood her up on her feet. "There. You think you can stand by yourself now?"

Eva nodded a bit more solemnly now, with Klaus's large hands gripping her small shoulders. As he looked down at her small face his grip became gentler. Not that he was being nice, he told himself, he just didn't want her distracted while he gave her instructions. "Think you can walk now without falling flat on your face now?" Eva nodded again and turned to walk away. Her sleeves were dragging, softly brushing over the cesspool of the ground, as she headed back to her hiding spot.

Klaus rolled his eyes in the dark. "Get "your ass back here!" Eva turned and watched as Klaus strode quickly the distance between them. He pulled out his knife as he walked.

"This is ridiculous!" He snatched the arm of her oversize shirt and yanked on it. His irritation and uncomfortableness had him yanking more than he had actually meant too. He found himself holding the sleeve of the shirt in one hand with the other sleeve dangling in the dirt at his feet. A very naked little girl stood in front of him.

He looked, almost in disbelief at the shirt in his hand and then at the girl once more. This time he noticed how emaciated the child appeared, and then again at how naked the poor child was, dark bruises marring her pale skin. "Quit staring at me! Turn around!" He barked.

Quickly and obediently the small waif did. This view was just as bad! Klaus turned his back to her too.

He pulled a section of the sleeve and sheared it off with his knife, repeating the same process with the other sleeve, muttering under his breath the entire time. "Damn scrawny ass kids! All big eyed and staring at staring at me with their stupidly long eyelashes waving away!"

He turned back around to the child, still muttering and looked at her back. The dark bruises from Rissling still showing just as grotesque as the marks on the other side of her. Gruffly he spoke again, "Turn around and keep your eyes closed!" Not knowing why, he bothered to say that he rolled his eyes and sighed. After all, she was the naked one, not he. He muttered again about his becoming an idiot tonight.

With the shirt firmly surrounding her once more, with her new sleeves- one ending at her wrist and the other at her elbow, she looked up at him again, a question in her eyes. Softer than he had ever spoke to her before, or ever would again he told himself, he bent to meet her eyes. "You remember what I said, kid?" Eva nodded and Klaus continued, "And don't you dare come slithering out of nowhere again and grab me!"

Eva shyly smiled, "Because you don't want me to scare you again Kraus!"

Klaus roughly, but not unkindly shoved her in the same direction as she had been heading before. He watched her pick up the bottom of her shirt as though it were a dress and step macabrely over the limb of a corpse, as though she were simply stepping over a bubbling creek in a field.

He whispered loudly at her small retreating back. "You didn't scare me! I was yawning!" It was mostly the truth, he had been yawning, but being caught in mid squeak had damaged his ego. She sure was a cheeky brat. He wasn't absolutely sure, nor would he admit to anyone, even himself but her spunk sort of enamored itself to him. Not much of course, he told himself again.

As he walked past the general direction of where she disappeared too he heard the smallest drawn out "squee-eeek" with a slight hiccup at the end. That little shit was over there hiccupping in laughter at him. Didn't she know he could kill her any second? Where the hell was her terror of him? She should have cried and screamed when he glared at her. Didn't she know he came to kill her?

He stomped back to his barracks to get away from the pint size source of all his angst this day. He had gone to kill the young witch, and had left thinking of mountain streams… "and probably flowers and butterflies and all that dumb shit too!" He continued muttering to himself as he walked. A god damned bleeding heart fool is what he was, chastising himself to keep from laughing out loud again.

Josef stepped back in the barracks a while after Klaus had returned. He sniffed the air as he pulled his hat off to set on the rack. Confused, he sniffed again; Klaus hated cooking with a passion. It was only something he did to keep himself from starving half to death. Klaus was standing at the sink, angrily chopping vegetables and throwing them into a boiling pot of broth on the stove.

Josef sat heavily, his heart guilty. He knew he had to say something to Klaus and try to explain his actions earlier. His choice had threatened the life of his friend and he was sorry.

He heard Klaus's footsteps approaching and took a breath, readying himself to speak. Klaus instead walked over and hit him in the back of the head with a broth covered ladle.

"I took care of it! Unpack your bags! You're not going anywhere, you damn fool!"

Josef rubbed the back of his head pulling his hand away to look at the broth and bring a cautious finger to his tongue to taste the stew, grimacing at the flavor. "Klaus I have to explain. I don't... I just don't know what happened. There was an old man and I almost felt like I didn't have a choice...it was as if he...as if she had..." he broke off, took a breath and readied himself to explain what he had stumbled over a moment before.

Klaus held up a hand. "I don't care and frankly I don't want to know" In reality, Klaus knew all too well what the hell Josef was trying to tell him. The same damn thing had happened to him too; Klaus however would never admit to it. "It's done. I took care of it. Now unpack your shit and keep an eye on the stew."

Josef knew his brother well enough to know he was withholding something. He could only hope that what his friend was withholding wasn't the message that he was to be shot for treason the next morning. Or worse yet was that this surprisingly 'more awful than normal' Klaus made stew wouldn't be his last meal.

Josef busied himself in the kitchen. In the couple months that he and Klaus had been in this barracks, Eva had become somewhat of a fixture. Although uncommon, often other Jews and even Jewish children were used as messengers. Usually they ended up in the ovens or the graves, but sometimes a wee bit of luck and some cleverness kept a few children alive. This was the case with Eva...and Josef kind of missed her light and airy presence in the corner of their barracks awaiting the next chore.

Many a survivor had walked out of these camps alive, saying that they did not live because they were better than anyone else, they simply were luckier. Thousands of years into the future people would still remember this time in his country's history and sadly shake their heads.

He looked over at Eva's corner and let out a sigh. She too had passed on the way so many, nearly all of the children had. He could only hope Klaus had been merciful and that the child's death had been quick. The child deserved that much respect at least.

Chapter 18

Quietly, once more the villagers had assembled at the fence. They would take another one or two of these hurting souls out. They had no idea, that for each of the prisoners they rescued, several more had been put to death. The guards assumed they knew where their brethren had gone and punished them however they saw fit that particular day.

Security patrols were more regular and methodical. A single pair of guards were charged with slowly and quietly walking the perimeter to find out how and where the few prisoners were escaping from. Of course the men in the towers were on high alert. On this night, Rissling himself would walk the perimeter. He hoped to find someone trying to escape, just to kill them. He was angry. If his guards couldn't keep the slovenly inmates from escaping, he sure as hell could.

As he paced the fence lines, his eyes darting left and right, looking for an errant striped uniform, he never noticed the dark hole under the fence or the dark shapes huddling beneath black cloth to hide them from view.

Henryck the blacksmith held his breath until after Rissling passed. He had only about 20 minutes before Rissling would pass again. That was only if Rissling was the only guard on tonight. Slowly he pushed one of the brave villagers, the young man named Dorek under the fence. The young man was to quickly crawl through the hole and dig it a bit deeper, while putting the extra dirt he removed into a cloth sack to drag out as to not leave any evidence behind. Then he would carefully use dirt, rocks and leaves to stake a cloth over the hole and make it look as though it were simply just a small pile of refuse and not an escape.

Dorek worked quickly knowing his life was at stake. He had been quick to volunteer at the second meeting. At first he had simply snuck into the blacksmiths shop to see what all the fuss was about. He had heard his mother muttering to herself about it. When he had heard what the plan was, he knew he would stand up with the men in his village and volunteer his time. They couldn't let a child do this job and he couldn't imagine trying to hide a hole as big as the blacksmiths shoulders. They would need a boulder to hide a hole big enough for the blacksmith. No, hiding a hole this size of him would be difficult enough.

He would help these people. His mother spoke against the villagers. She along with her friend Antone plotted to end the villagers plan, but they would go through regardless of what his mother and Antone thought. Many of his friends who showed the same "tendencies" as his mother called it, as he himself had toward the same sex had been killed. He was not going to let that happen to anyone else if he could help it. Several from his village had been killed, some had been his best friends.

He didn't know at this very moment, his mother Susi was walking towards the entrance to the camp. She would single-handedly thwart this plan to put her town in danger, not realizing her own son was in the most danger as she self-righteously marched on down the road towards the front gate of Majdanek.

He had just seen a thin young man running towards him, silently crying in thanks and crawled through the hole to help him. The villagers had told him, in no uncertain terms that no matter what he did; do NOT crawl through and into the second fence! Dorek was not going to stay safely behind that fence and not help this young man. He was going to save this young man, or he would die trying.

Henryck was livid. He saw his young villager, Dorek run inside the camp fence towards the escaping young man and pull him towards the hole in the fence. As the kid and the inmate reached the fence, Henryck noticed some lights coming on inside the main guard tower at the entrance. Something had the guards awake and moving around. "Hurry up! They're coming!" he whispered to Dorek.

The inmate came first, moaning at the effort to push his body through the hole. Henryck, and then his wife grabbed the man's wrists and pulled him out. The assembled villagers behind him quickly pulled him back farther and wrapped him in a dark cloth. Two of the men each grabbed and arm and a leg and began running with the young man. Four more villagers, two by two, took off running behind the men. They would relay this poor prisoner to safety.

Dorek came through the hole in the fence as quickly and carefully as he could while pulling the cloth back into place and showering it with dirt to hopefully cover the evidence of the escape. As soon as he made it past the second fence line Beatrice yanked his arms quite roughly and began dragging him towards the village. Henryck wasted no time in covering up the hole on his side of the fence. He saw the flashlights running towards him, and could only hope that he had done a good enough job of hiding the escape hatch.

He slowly backed away from the fence keeping the black cloth wrapped tightly around him to keep from uncovering him too much and be seen. He met Beatrice and Dorek in a stand of trees that would hopefully keep them from the prying eyes and searching flashlights of the Nazi guards inside the death camp fences. As the flashlights moved past the spot in the fence, Dorek, Henryck and Beatrice began running toward the village.

Before the limits of the village, Henryck was just about to grab Dorek and give him a stern talking too when they heard footsteps on the road. He quietly pulled the young man to him and hid him under his black cloth as best he could. For as scrawny as the kid was, he sure was tall. Henryck pushed hard down on Dorek's shoulder to get him to hide. He and Beatrice slowly sank as far as they could to the ground, hoping that they would not be found.

As the wandering form came past on the road, Beatrice and Henryck met eyes. The young man stiffened as he peeked out from behind the dark cloth. Despite the strong blacksmiths hand tight on the kids arm, all but demanding he remain silent, Dorek wrenched free from the grip and marched up to the woman. She jumped at the rustle in the bushes and held a hand to her mouth as she recognized her son stomping towards her.

"Mother! What have you done? You have put us all in danger!" The kid ran to his mother and looked as though he didn't even know her. Perhaps he never did. She sure didn't know him at all.

"What are you doing?" She screeched at him, and reached to slap his face. The young man grabbed his mother's arm and held it away from him. He might look slight but he was strong. He overpowered her swing and held her arm out from her body, just because he could...and maybe just to show her the man he had become while she hadn't been noticing him, if she ever had.

"Mother they murdered my friends. I'm not going to let them murder anyone else if I can help it!"

"Your friends were nothing but trash, Dorek. Mutants. It was necessary!" Susi yelled back at him, her voice rising to dangerous levels on the exposed road.

"Mother. I too am a mutant. You would have me suffer the same fate as those innocents?"

Susi stumbled backwards as though her son had struck her, dramatically placing her hand over her heart. "No! You can't be!"

In the cover of the darkness on the side of the road, Beatrice and Henryck exchanged a couple of grimaces and eye-rolls at the overly dramatic Susi.

"Mother, I am. I don't care what you think anymore, as you don't care what I think. I will continue saving these people if I can. I will not sit and be a part of these murders. You can be; if you feel so strongly about letting innocent people die for *your* ignorance."

He turned and stalked away, leaving his mother standing in the road, confused. Slowly she turned and followed her son back to the village.

Long after the woman left, Henryck and Beatrice followed. "I knew that all along you know." Henryck said, matter of factly.

"You did not you big ox! You're the one always wondering when young Dorek would be getting married to one of the village girls."

"Well, yeah. He needed a cover story! Don't be a goose." Henryck elbowed his woman.

Beatrice rolled her eyes and sighed. This big ox had had no idea, but he sure liked to pretend he was right all the time. She'd let him pretend again. They had saved another soul. They were still in danger, but another person was alive because of them and the couple's mood was buoyant.

"I know you knew, you big galoot." Beatrice smiled up at her man. He looked back down at her, his wonderfully brave wife with a smile in his eyes.

"Maybe…uh…you might get one of those kinds of feelings too" he winked and elbowed her again, raising his bushy eyebrows up and down at her.

She rolled her eyes up at him again. "Get yourself and your fuzzy mind back home. None of that talk now, you overgrown weasel!"

They laughed again and turned towards their shop, brushing arms as they walked comfortably together in the darkness. Tomorrow was another day. They would wait a few days though, until the officer's guard was down and they wouldn't be out patrolling in full force. They would save more. Dorek would save many more with them. They had a good system in place and would continue as long as they could.

Chapter 19

It was hours later in the dark of the night when Klaus came back from his rounds. They had been unusually busy. A villager had come to the gates and said the other villagers were planning to escape with some of the Jewish prisoners. The guards had all ran around to find spots in the fence, or movement outside of the fence. They hadn't found any, but they would all be out in full force looking for a place of escape or places where it looked as though villagers had been coming to the fence.

It wouldn't be easy. No one ever caught them, but there were usually a few new trails in the grass. The villagers would quite often sneak food items to whatever inmate they happened to be able to see. It was a constant irritation to the guards. At some times, they would look the other way, but usually the officers were enraged that some villager who probably belonged in this camp was on the outside sneaking food in!

Even in his half asleep state, Josef wondered why Klaus was being unusually quiet as he shut and locked the front door. Normally, Klaus walked in stomping around, talking to himself and yelling about his day before slurping down his dinner and heading off to bed. Josef's thoughts quickly wandered from Klaus and back to a fitful sleep full of an old man whispering to save a child.

Josef had no idea how much time had passed or how long he had been asleep again, but he slowly woke to the feeling that he was being watched. In his dream the old man's accusing eyes were steadfast on his own. In his own bed as he was waking up, the same feeling of eyes drilling into his own was overwhelming. He slowly opened his eyes to find a pair of brown eyes mere inches from his nose.

It was Eva, or rather Eva's ghost staring directly into his eyes, looking as though she were in the flesh. Klaus already told him he took care of her. He quickly sat up and yelled as he scooted away from the apparition standing at the head of his bed. The blankets tangled as tried to scoot backwards to the farthest side of his bed nearest the wall. His weight slid his bed from away from the wall and his body fell in between his bed and the wall. He struggled to pull the covers off of his head.

From Klaus's bed he heard Klaus's deep laugh, "She scared the shit out of you!" Eva giggled and Josef took a deep steadying breath, while holding a hand over his heart. Eva laughed, her brown eyes twinkling in the low light of the room.

"There. I took care of it. Now you feed the damn thing and find it a place to sleep. And leave me out of your bullshit after this!" Klaus reached up to shut off his light and rolled over, pulling the wool blanket up to his shoulders.

Josef had been focused on Eva's eyes and hadn't noticed before, but he realized her hair had been shorn off. Besides her girlish face, the rest of her looked like a boy...well, a slight boy with a terrible haircut, that is. Slowly he untangled all his limbs from his sheets and blankets and crawled up and out of the space behind his bed.

He grabbed a piece of her now short hair and gave it a small tug. Eva whispered softly, conspiratorially to Josef, "Kraus said I still looked like a silly little girl, so he cut it and then he threw into the fire. Now I look like a boy."

Klaus muttered, not moving, his face still smashed into his pillow. "I figured it would be easier for you to finish 'it' with her not looking like herself. Now you might as well go feed it *for tonight only*! Oh and you, kid! Shut up now!"

Josef chuckled for a second, then became more serious as he looked at the child. Klaus was right, he did have to finish the job, to at least do something with her...But right now he could at least give her a bowl of stew and put her to bed. He could kill her anytime tomorrow. Klaus was right...if they were caught with her they would both be court martialed and probably hung- or worse.

Eva ate her stew and sweetly thanked Josef for the good food. Before Josef could let her know he was not to blame for the awful food Klaus spoke again, his voice still muffled by his pillow, sounding half asleep. "I cooked that stupid stew.

Don't let that ass take any of the credit for it. He didn't do shit but put it in a bowl so you could stuff your face."

"It was good Kraus" the small voice replied.
"Shut up and quit your damn yammering!"
"Ok Kraus"
"Shut that damn yowling stray up, Josef!"
"Ok Klaus!" Josef spoke up
As Klaus answered, "Fuck you!" Josef pantomimed the words he knew would be coming from his friend's mouth. He winked at Eva and got a smile in return.

Eva smiled and yawned. Josef took her dish and washed it quickly. He made sure to dry and put it away, so there would be no evidence of a third person in the cabin.

Josef returned to his bunk to find Eva standing upright, but leaning on his bunk fast asleep, soft snores emitting from her small nose and slightly open mouth. Josef stood a moment longer, watching and listening as the child slept, oblivious to the very real danger she was *still in*.

He chanced a glance at Klaus to find his friends steel grey eyes hard on his own. "You are a god damned idiot, that's what you are." Klaus rolled over to face the wall, pulling his blanket back to his shoulder, leaving Josef to figure out what to do with their tiny prisoner turned house guest. The bright young girl that could get them all killed with a single word to anyone else. A fine predicament he had gotten them into. He was an idiot, that much was damn sure, but he wasn't a killer.

Killing her would eliminate all of the problems he was facing. Now, asleep with a full belly in this warm room would be perfect. A pillow over her face, and he and Klaus wouldn't be in this mess that he created. Looking down at her face, with the slightly upturned nose, he realized he couldn't go through that any better than he had before and look where that had gotten him.

Klaus could still kill her. In fact, he was sure that's what Klaus had meant when he said he had taken care of it earlier. If Klaus did kill her or if he was going to kill her, Josef wouldn't stop him. He couldn't. He was the one who singlehandedly had brought this danger upon them. Josef had no idea of the issues Klaus had had when he went specifically to kill the child earlier that night.

He wouldn't want to see it happen, but they were Waffen-SS, the best of the best. They couldn't be found harboring a Jewish kid everyone thought dead, no matter how cute she snored. They couldn't keep a child hidden in their barracks that the entire staff 'knew was dead'. This troublesome, yet adorable girl was a death sentence in the making. It was entirely all his fault. Josef and his bleeding heart… he sure knew how to make things difficult.

With a soft sigh, he got up and grabbed an extra blanket, wrapping it around her, Indian style, before gathering her small body into his arms. He laid her gently on his bed as far as he could put her near the wall. Carefully, as not to wake the child he was just contemplating killing, he pulled his own blanket out from underneath her. An idiot. A god damned idiot.

He lay awake in his bed for a while longer, not able to sleep. Upon closing his eyes, he saw the face of the old man. The seeping wound, the graying hair matted on one side and the angry, yet solemn eyes of the old man condemning him; accusing him. He lay awake, eyes open, listening to the camp. The occasional shriek, the moaning, an occasional gun shot or two, conversations of guards as they past near his barrack and far off in the distance he heard the rail cars, rumbling like thunder; carrying its load of innocent children just like Eva, bound for death.

He realized then, he could not and would not kill this innocent baby. This child; his child now, would live.

As his eyes fluttered and finally closed, the last thing Josef saw or remembered was the old man's face. It was smiling at him, the grey hair soft and clean, lifting in the wind, his face now whole and unblemished. The old man smiled again, nodded, and turned to walk away vanishing slowly into a light colored fog.

Chapter 20

Hanna had woke, the day after her child's death curled up next to Marta on their bunk. Her first waking thought was to reach her hand out to find her baby and pull her close in an embrace only to realize and remember that her child was dead. As the precious liquid tears rolled from her eyes, she heard a tapping on the wall near her corner bunk, her home in hell. She had been in this bunk for over ten months now. The tapping sounded again and then a very hushed whisper. Marta awoke and the women exchanged nervous glances.
"Hanna"
Hanna slowly reached a hand out to the wall. She met Marta's eyes again as she hesitantly tapped back on the wall, replying in a stuttering whisper. "Ye...yes"

"Your child lives" in German, and footsteps moved away from her wall, gravel crunching beneath the heavy sounding feet.

Marta put an arm around Hanna's shoulders, "Oh Hanna... I'm so sorry. What a terrible and cruel thing to do." Marta pulled her friend closer for a tight hug. "I'm so sorry Hanna. Oh God, I'm so sorry. They are even crueler than I could have ever imagined."

Hanna sat as far back in the corner of her bunk as she could. She pulled her knees up to her chest and wrapped her arms around them and lay her head atop. She cried with what little strength she had left. Those murderers had not only killed her child in cold blood, but then they came back to taunt her about it afterward.

Josef walked away from the women's barracks. He had felt it almost a duty to inform Eva's mother that her child lived. Certainly this would help her, help her grief and keep her strong. He never imagined for a moment, that Hanna would see his 'confession' as a cruel joke. He couldn't have known the pain that went through her heart at hearing those words. Josef saw cruelty every day. He saw the suffering every day, but had not lived it. He was removed from it, although he felt he was a part of it and could sympathize.

He just assumed that telling her would help her. He had no idea the opposite was true. He just knew that he could tell her. No one would believe her if she talked anyway. Who would believe a distraught Jewish mother that ran up and said, "A disembodied voice told me through my barracks wall that my child was still alive!", when nearly all of the staff had seen the child dead and buried. Anyone who hadn't physically seen it had surely heard of it.

As Josef continued his rounds, preparing to head to his assigned duties of the morning, he wasn't apprehensive about leaving Eva with Klaus. If he killed her, there wasn't much he could do about it. She would either live or she wouldn't. He actually kind of liked the girl, but he couldn't force his friend to take the fall for his weakness. She would simply live or die.

He still had a nagging feeling that there was something Klaus wasn't telling him, besides what he already knew and that was Klaus brought the child back. What he didn't know was why...unless Klaus planned to use her to show that he himself had not followed orders and had essentially committed treason. It just didn't make sense. Klaus was cooking, something he never did, left to kill the child and came back with her in tow...with a brand new *horrible* haircut.

Josef's thoughts continued throughout the morning and well into the afternoon. He was in charge of yet another pit dig. This one had been ordered to be more than 20 feet deep and nearly three times that long. He worked for most of the day, stopping briefly while the men ate lunch. Some of the guards just ate right there, next to the inmates, sometimes with the dead stacked just meters from where they were eating. Josef could never stand the thought of eating in the yards, much less actually eating in front of the dead and the dying.

Josef was the next decade or the next generation older than most of the young soldiers. These young men had lived only with the regimes doctrines. Josef himself remembered a motherland that was not exactly thriving, but it was also not in the murdering business. This went beyond war. This was cold blooded murder. It was genocide. Josef, being at only one camp in his military career, had no idea how widespread the genocide actually was.

It would be said again and again years later, how many of the German soldiers had no idea how widespread the camps were. Many were kept in the dark with their orders, not realizing what they were going to be doing until they arrived.

Some guards had run off, knowing it was treason and a death sentence. Some guards did as little as possible with the running of the camps. Some sat and cried like old women when they discovered the true barbarity of the crimes being committed in the name of a true race.

Others though, they truly reveled in it. They had all the power in the world. The more torture, the more they enjoyed it. Those true barbarians were what Josef despised. They were brutal and enjoyed every moment of their 'work'. Josef also despised the men like him. Decent men that would die if they spoke, so they said nothing; perhaps discreetly helping a Jew escape now and then if they knew they could get away with it.

It seemed as though, whatever the latest atrocity to occur was, there was always some...and sometimes many more that were quick to embrace it, to expound upon it and go one farther. It was simply a game to some; a horrible game of life, and of death.

Thousands of his countrymen believed implicitly in the regime. Those same were set to inherit a Germany that Josef remembered as tough, but happy. His country would never be the same. None of them would ever be the same. He had no knowledge that the entire world would *never* be the same.

Josef wasn't aware that the Nazi regime was nearing its end. The word that trickled down to him was that Germany was defeating all of the allies that dared to step foot on its hallowed soil. All he knew was that life as he knew it was over, nearing an end, as it already had for millions of men, women and children; nearly all of them innocent.

When the hours he had pulled that day ended, he headed to his barracks. He was ready for a hot meal and a shower. When he stepped onto his porch, he paused for a moment. He would find out if the child were dead or not today. He waited another second longer before he turned the knob…which didn't turn.

A noise from inside had Josef pulling his hand off the knob and stood at attention. Not a full salute, but at attention, not knowing who was on the other side of his door. It may very well be his court martial and one very dead child in his kitchen. Evidence of his treason to his own mother land.

The door was flung open and an angry looking Klaus stood in the open doorway glaring at him. "It's about time you idiot. I've got shit to do, and you come just strolling up "Klaus's eyes flashed angrily. "Well quit standing on the step like a dumbass. You're drawing attention to yourself."

Josef stepped inside the door as Klaus shoved passed him, already yelling at the first prisoner he saw walking toward the other guard barracks. "Aren't you supposed to be doing something? Walk faster and get out of my sight!"

Josef closed the door and walked into the kitchen. There was no sign of Eva, but there was certainly a mess in the kitchen. Some kind of nasty smelling burnt food was stuck to a pan on the stove, while flour covered the counter. An egg lay drying in a cracked puddle on the floor and a half raw slab of salt pork lay in a pile of grease near the back of the stove.

Josef surveyed the scene, confused, before he headed into his bedroom. Josef's bed appeared untouched with the exception of his two best white shirts lying in a pile wadded up.

Klaus's bed though was another story. The blankets and pillows were strewn around the bed and a deep pile of Klaus's clothes were piled in the far corner of his bed abutting the wall. Eva was gone.

Josef sighed and unbuttoned his jacket, pulling it off and then his undershirt beneath it. He unbuckled his belt and began to pull it through his belt loops when the pile on Klaus's bed moved and a small snicker came from inside it.

He moved first to the window to look out, then back through the front room to lock the front door. Assuring himself that no one could come in and that there wasn't anyone within hearing distance he walked back toward the bedroom, pausing only to strip off his boots by the table and tiptoe back into the room.

Although Josef was far from experienced with anything at all that had to do with a child, he stood at Klaus's bed looking down at the suspicious pile of clothes. "I thought I heard Klaus's bed laughing at me!" He felt completely out of his element, trying to play make believe and interact with the small child. Her life was totally in his hands now. By his hasty decision a day before, he changed her life...and his own.

His happy bachelor and Top SS status changed to that of a surrogate father/uncle figure and should anyone discover his secret; a wanted fugitive. Sometimes he gave himself the most annoying problems. Thus far, that's what Eva was. Josef hadn't stopped to think over much about the implications of his decision. He knew he would have plenty of time to think of nothing but the child in the coming days, for now though...he had to find a child.

A smiling child, a bright ray of sunshine on the stormiest of days; hiding in a pile of clothes. If he did nothing else, maybe he could make her last few days on earth, nothing but fun...and food.

The pile in front of him barely moved and Josef quickly grabbed a shirt off the top. He yanked it off the pile as though a magician trying to leave the glasses untouched by pulling the tablecloth out from underneath. He saw a small hand exposed for a split second before it disappeared back into the pile of clothing.

He pulled two handfuls of clothing up quickly. Eva sat in the center of the pile only the top of her bare shoulders visible. He threw the clothes back over her when he realized she probably didn't have any clothes on.

"Why don't you have any clothes on?"

"Oh. Kraus said I was quite stinky and made me take a shower. He washed me so much my face hurt badly and it got all red. He was making me new clothes when you came back. Then he yelled at me again when you touched the door and threw all his clothes out of his trunk on me."

Josef looked at the small face in the pile, and then back to his best shirts lying on his bed. "Eva...where are the new clothes Klaus was making for you?" Eva pointed to his shirts on his bed. Josef walked over and picked up his best and favorite shirt first. He held it out in front of him. The entire collar that had once settled perfectly around his neck was cut completely off. He realized that a large perfect square that used to ride over his honed chest was gone too. He held the shirt and looked at Eva, an eyebrow raised in question.

"Kraus said I needed underwear."

Eva stood quickly and turned in a circle. Josef now realized the child wasn't as naked as he had previously thought. His best uniform necktie was wrapped crisscross around her slight chest. The missing part of his best shirt was fashioned into what he could only call a loincloth.

The collar of his shirt was wrapped around her miniscule waist. The missing front of his shirt, where the square hole was now, was looped under and was tucked in the back of the seam of his collar behind her, a flap hanging over in the back. Josef sat on his bed and laughed. Angry that his stupid friend cut his best shirts up, but glad the bright child was still here. Tears of laughter were threatening to leak out of his eyes as he fumbled around beside him for his other good shirt.

He held that one aloft too, to survey the damage. This shirt had precisely half of one of his best, and only extra, shoelaces tied in the middle of the bottom hem of his shirt, creating two distinct holes. As he turned his good shirt around he saw the back of his shirt had a slit from the collar to about six inches down the back. The one end of his collar had the other half of his good shoelace tied onto it.

Josef looked at the child, cocked and eyebrow "What the hell is this?"

"Kraus said it was my new suit. He said I needed something not stinky, so he used your shirts"

Eva walked over and trustingly placed her hand on his shoulder and lifted a small foot in the air. He looked again at his good shirt and shrugged. There was nothing he could do now. The damage to his shirts was done. He held his shirt open and she stepped into it. As she put her arms in through the arm holes of his old T-shirt, she turned her back to him to tie it.

After he fiddled with tying the shoelace on the opposite side of the collar to his liking he put his hands down. Eva turned around. "Now you tie your tie here" she pointed to her waist. Josef groaned and spun Eva back around to undo the bow he had just painstakingly tied in his shirt collar.

Once his tie was removed from her chest under his shirt, he wrapped it around her waist and looked over his handiwork. He had to admit Klaus had come up with a clever idea, albeit at the expense of his best shirts.

Eva walked back to Klaus's bunk, the hem of his shirt dangling between her legs awkwardly and terribly inappropriately with every small step, Josef burst into a round of laughter. This was definitely a design flaw in need of some help.

As she sat on the bed and looked at Josef with her long lashed eyes, he remembered the mess in the kitchen. "So what happened out there?" He hooked a thumb towards the kitchen.

"Kraus yelled and said he knew you would ditch him like a bitch and…" Josef held his hands up to stop her. Only a few hours with the kid and already she was picking up on Klaus's foul language.

"Bitch probably isn't a word you should say, Eva." Although he didn't know why he didn't want her cursing, for all that she had seen and lived through the last months or years of her life. He simply didn't want that small bit of innocence corrupted.

"Oh." She thought for a moment, her short, newly clean toes wiggling off the end of Klaus bunk. She smiled and with a casual shrug of her shoulders, answered Josef once again, "Well, he also said you were a stupid fu—"

"Whoa! Stop right there." Josef got up and walked into the kitchen to survey the mess again. He walked back in a moment later, a dish cloth in his hands. He tried a different tactic to find out what happened this time, his earlier line of questioning not working out so well for him. "So Eva, what did Klaus try to cook?"

Eva jumped off the bed and walked into the kitchen; she shrugged, looked around and said, "Just some God damned breakfast."

Chapter 21

Of all the horrors Hanna had witnessed and had endured, nothing was as bad as this. Nothing could have compared to, nor prepared her for the crushing emptiness she now felt.

She entered the kitchen via the back hall entrance, her arms already full of the fresh vegetables she would have to cook for the monsters today, while her fellow inmates would drink cold broth and a piece of bread- if they were lucky. If only she had access to poison. She would kill the lot of them, of course she would die, but life held no more reason, no more value to her.

She jumped and tensed when she heard and felt the measured steps behind her, but she didn't turn around. Every once in a while you would run into some of the guards who did not want you to look at them at all. They seemed afraid you might see sympathy and pity in their eyes. Other guards, a majority of them wanted you to see the hate and disgust as they regarded you as nothing more than some vermin to be destroyed by any means.

It was better not to look at all until you were sure of what you were supposed to do. She tensed more when she felt hands grip her hips roughly and pull her back into the body behind her. The hands moved up to her ribs, then higher and squeezed hard bruising her soft flesh. "Too bad Josef and Klaus killed your squalling rat before I could. I would have had fun killing her."

The hands squeezed harder before she was released and roughly shoved away from the Commander and into the counter in front of her. He shoved her hard again before striding from the room.

Oh, why had she been made to suffer through this terrible life without her baby? How could she possibly continue on without her child? It was as though the loss of her only child filled her, completely consumed her entire being. Her will to live was all but gone. She hurt so much.

She knew she had to keep going forth. She knew she couldn't let her child's death be in vain. Maybe, if she tried to will herself to survive, she could somehow live. She could fight to find the will to survie, to share the atrocities she had seen and suffered here. She could tell the entire world about her small but tough Eva and how strong she was, right to the very end. She could tell them of how brave she was, never complaining and how much joy she brought to her mother.

Hanna put her elbows on the counter and bent down. She placed her forehead on her arms and cried.

Later that evening after roll call she lay in her bunk. Marta had come in, freshly bruised again and the women held each other tightly. Marta lay awake long after Hanna fell into what she hoped would be a healing sleep. She curled against Hanna's back and wrapped the blanket around them. Then they slept, taking comfort in each other's closeness.

Very few prisoners noticed, and if they did, they pretended to be asleep as the SS guard walked between the rows of bunks. The guard made his way to the corner bunk and stopped. He only stood a moment longer and then moved on, but not before tossing a couple pieces of bread near the sleeping women. Marta awoke a few moments later and silently awoke Hanna with a light touch on her shoulder. Both women smiled at their unheard of good fortune and un-wrapped the still warm bread, not knowing who their benefactor had been. It certainly wasn't the best bread, and wasn't even sure it could be considered bread, but it was sustenance…and someone cared enough to help them, even if they couldn't cook.

Rissling was pissed. Josef and Klaus always seemed to get in his way. He could have taken the Jewish whore this morning in his kitchen, but her spirit was practically dead since her precious daughter was killed only last month. There would have been no challenge in that. Rissling needed the conquest, the challenge and the physical exertion. He was a top predator! Hanna would have been no sporting challenge.

There was however, a great conquest in forcing a young man who should have been in his prime to submit to his demands, no matter what they may have been. The game he played was a dangerous one. Well, dangerous only for him. It was fatal for his chosen victims. After a near brush with death several years ago, he made sure to choose his next victims carefully. Once he had been too excited and chosen a man who very nearly overpowered him. He had been forced to pull his boot knife and kill the prisoner to save his own life. It had not only scared him, but had infuriated him.

Not that it mattered that he killed the prisoner, he killed all of them, but he liked to do it when he wanted to, not when he had too.

He always made sure his next chosen victims were chosen precisely the same way. For about three days they were worked hard, with less bread and broth than usual. On the third day he would look them over at morning roll call. If he miscalculated and they were too weak and sickly looking he simply shot them in line for any reason he could think of. It was of no consequence to him. Why feed something if they weren't worth the feed? If they were still in top form, he simply put them back to work and regular rations. There was no point to killing a working machine and absolutely no point in putting himself in any real danger.

He may look them up again, but usually when he passed, he simply never thought of them again. This was the same as after he used them and killed them. They simply never entered his mind again. They were of no consequence. They never would be. They never had been to Rissling and thousands of the same ilk as himself.

The ones he passed on though, they were the lucky ones. They may have known they were being targeted for something, all prey animals had a sense they were being hunted-even humans still carry that innate skill. But when nothing happened after a while, they went on living as best they could, beautifully oblivious to the death that had been stalking them at least in one form. One could not escape death though in a prison hell such as this.

It was heaven for Rissling.

It was just such a reason Hanna had been spared. Had she turned and fought him, he may not have held back, or been able to hold back. Rissling considered himself a hunter. When his prey fought back or tried to escape, that's when he unsheathed his claws. He made a fist and punched his other hand, wincing only slightly when he hit it. He was in his top form and a top predator. Today he would go hunting.

This morning though he was on a hunt. It had been a while since his last victim and he was feeling the itch again. This time though he had a different prey in mind. At the terrific fight Eva had put up, he found himself wanting to experience a different prey. He watched a young Jew named Jules working. Rissling remembered but few of the Jewish pig's names. Those that interested him in one form or another were always remembered by name however. The rest were simply inconsequential. They mattered not. They never would. They never will. Rissling smiled and headed out the door.

This particular day, he was searching for the man named Jules. Specifically, he wanted Jules's younger brother or his brother's bratty friend. They were all brats! Either one of them would make him a good evening's entertainment if they survived that long. It was a choice that also saved time! He wouldn't have to wait to wear down an older and stronger person. He almost clapped with glee, his trap set. If he hunted the youngest of the herd, he would never again have to wait to wear down an older, stronger one.

After he had lost his opportunity to 'take good care of Eva' by that damn Klaus, he couldn't get that feeling out of his system. He wanted to see just how far he could go. Some of his guards would be downright disquieted, almost hostile if they knew his plans. Some would have gladly joined in, he knew they would, but this was his sport. He couldn't wait to begin, and now he never had to wait again if he didn't want to.

If he told a guard to get him a new messenger boy to replace Eva, and said boy just happened to die a day or so later, well...he died. None would be the wiser. None would care. No one would ask.

With that settled he turned to get out of the disgusting yard. He smiled as he walked. All he had to do was signal a guard and one of the stinking rats would be delivered to him quickly on almost a silver platter. The hunt would be on, and he wouldn't even have to lift a finger.

Before he returned to his barracks to await his prize, he decided to swing by Klaus and Josef's and get their upcoming meeting set up. He finally decided to tell them he got his transfer papers and he was ready to get out of here. All he had left to do was get their paperwork delivered and signed. He could sport a few more times before he left though.

He knocked on their door and heard shuffling feet inside before the door was thrust open. Josef stood looking at him, a cup of coffee in one hand and a mouthful of buttered bread. This lot sure was disrespectful. No matter, Rissling wasted no time. "Come to my barracks tomorrow at 3pm. We need to finish getting the command turned over. My release papers have arrived."

Josef nodded his assent and turned to walk back into his barracks. "Oh and since you deprived me of my messenger, bring me another one; a boy this time. He will begin working post haste." Rissling spoke and then stepped off the porch, entwining his fingers and pushing his arms out to snap them all at once. He was heading to his own barracks to prepare for his evening's entertainment.

Josef nodded again and shut the door. That sick bastard! Josef had no other recourse but to let Klaus know he was heading out. He knew exactly, or at least somewhat what Rissling had planned, but with a direct order, he could not disobey it, Rissling still outranked them, the fact that his transfer papers had arrived several weeks past. They were set to finally have free rein to run this place very soon, and he was not completely in charge yet. "I'll be back in a few minutes. That monster wants me to bring him a child."

Klaus was already lacing up his boots. "I heard him. I'll go do it. You find something to eat for that silly, mangy stray cat in there."

Without even waiting for a reply Klaus strode out the door. Josef stood in the doorway watching his friend walk away and toward the camp. Klaus had known Josef would hate himself for picking out any child, so he went and did it himself. In a heated argument, fueled by some of Germany's best whiskey once, he had accused Klaus of having no heart.

He had immediately regretted it, and regretted it again now as he watched his brother walk away to complete a task he had been assigned to. A terrible task that when completed, he wouldn't be able to look at himself in the same again. Klaus was no heartless bastard, but one hell of a damn good friend…even if he was a hard ass sometimes. Well, Josef smiled, most of the time. Yes…most of the time Klaus was just a jerk.

Chapter 22

Josef went back into his room. He spoke softly, sadly as he watched Eva crawl out from under Klaus's bunk. The men had placed spare clothes and towels under each of their bunks in the farthest corner. Eva was to hide underneath the closest one at the first sound of anyone entering the barracks.

He knew the smart girl had some great listening ears. She must have already spent at least a quarter, or more, of her life in camps like this. He wasn't exactly sure how much, but he did know that to some extent she had overheard and known what Rissling was asking for.

As he looked at the child standing at his feet, he didn't know what to say. How could he explain the atrocities his own people were committing? How could he explain how some needed more and more depravity every time? How did uncles and fathers explain such things to their children?

Eva came to him and crawled into his lap, her nose sniffing from the suppressed tears. He realized she was holding her tears back. She had been taught not to cry! Why that in and of itself bothered him, he wasn't exactly sure. It just did. It seemed such a small thing, but to take away the right to a child's tears… He shook his head and looked down at the top of her small head, her faced pressed tightly against his shirt, no trace of a tear on her thin cheeks. When she tilted her head back just enough to meet his eyes with her own so full of pain, he finally knew what to do. He let his heart guide him.

He gathered her close to him, stroking her hair lightly and rocking her. "It's ok Eva. It's ok to cry. I wish I could protect your little ears more, along with the rest of you."

Her sweet voice floated to his ears as he felt her hand patting his shoulder. "It's ok Josef. Momma says things have to be as hard as hard can be before they can ever be right again."

"Oh honey" He held her closer and continued rocking, feeling like crying himself. While she still never cried, when she began to relax in his arms, he smiled. The small girl felt nice in his arms, Eva felt natural, right. As if this had been what he had been missing his entire life, a child. His own small child. He smiled down at her, his voice deadly serious "There's something else very important we need to talk about though" he said, changing the subject. She met his eyes, crinkling up her nose, knowing from his tone that Josef had something up his sleeve.

"We haven't cooked anything for dinner yet and Klaus is going to come back in here hungrier, more irritated and louder than a big 'ol wild hog if we don't have some food ready!"

Eva looked up and smiled. "And smellier too?"

"Probably!" He tousled her hair, pulling on a couple of longer strands lightly. In just the last month with food, water and a dry, warm place to sleep she had already begun to gain some weight and her hair already had a few new silky strands beginning to grow. Josef decided that he would find his scissors and trim her hair a little more uniformly. It was a terrible haircut Klaus had given her with his boot knife the day he brought her home.

Her face, once so pale with dry skin patches had already begun to almost glow with the face a child should have. Well...that and Klaus's almost steady reminders to shower.

Klaus had eventually related to Josef that he had ended up forcefully carrying Eva into the shower that first day with all his clothes on just to get her in the shower stall and clean. "I had to get her in there with my hand over her mouth to keep her from screaming. Then Eva, bit me too!" Klaus had laughed at the memory and unconsciously rubbed his hand.

Once Eva discovered that this was not 'the bad shower' and she wasn't going to be hurt or worse, she ran right in at Klaus's reminders. Klaus just impatiently said, "If I have to suffer the company of a mangy kitten, it's going to be a clean mangy kitten!" To anyone else, Klaus's mannerisms were borderline cruel. To Josef, well...it was about as nice as his friend ever got. To Eva, bless her heart, every curse word Klaus directed at her could have been whispered sweet nothing. He liked her. She knew it. She felt it. Klaus didn't even know it himself, but Eva did. She remembered him. She knew him.

Josef went and busied himself in the kitchen, leaving Eva in the bedroom. Only when both men were present was Eva allowed to leave the bedroom and walk around. It was too dangerous for all of them if she were to be discovered. With only one of the men, they couldn't risk the door being flung open if Eva were to be in the room with them. With both of them, one could walk around masking the child's steps while the other came to the door in their own time.

One of these days, they would actually have to have an open discussion about what to do to keep the child safe. Thus far, they each talked to her and to each other, but they never talked about what to do with her. Klaus would not be happy, but Josef hoped he would at least pitch in a few ideas than what they had already done to if not ensure her safety, to at least keep them from being caught.

It was a long overdue discussion, from a problem Josef had created. He hoped that Klaus was fine with the child being there, he had seemed to be anyway. Perhaps, bringing up the child's fate was just pushing things too far. Klaus hadn't seemed to bother with it, he hadn't said anything. Maybe leaving things alone was the way to go. He would leave the discussion to Klaus. If he wanted to talk about it, they would. If not, they would just go on, each pretending that the child didn't exist.

Chapter 23

Klaus stomped angrily through the camp. Of all the damned duties he had ever been assigned to carry out, this one was the most incomprehensible. The only direct order he would ever purposefully disobey if he could. Even when it came to 'cleaning out' the ghetto and sending children to a camp, and yeah, once in a while shooting some to keep them from getting away, it hadn't mattered. What mattered was he was a patriot! Fighting for his mother land! He was a damn good soldier and he did as he was asked to!

He continued his musing while he walked, continuously searching for a child to fill the 'order'. Back then, it hadn't mattered. He, as many of his fellow soldiers, had been in the dark about what kind of camps they were sending people too. Most of them had been told work they were simply work camps and his men had even seen films showing the Jews blissfully working. Rounding them up had been nothing but a pain in the hind end. Didn't they see he was bringing them to a working camp? Sure, yeah… it wasn't your home, but follow orders!

None of the men in his battalion had known the true nature of the camps, nor the sheer numbers of them. There had been a few rumors, but they were all dismissed as Allied forces propaganda. That damn United States was just putting their nose where it didn't belong and spreading rumors about his countrymen, killing innocent people. Sure, sometimes they had to kill some as they were rounding them up, but they were only Jew's and there was nowhere near the amount the Allied forces were trying to claim.

Now though, he knew the difference. Then it had been many, and there had been many of his fellow soldiers with him. This time he knew the brutality and cruelty… and he was to find one single child to bring to slaughter; by himself alone. He would have a hand in this next child's death. Was the child, the girl safe and protected in his barracks, enough to make up for what he had to do now?

To drag a kid to the Camp Commander that he knew would abuse the child in ways that soldiers didn't even talk about, and they sure talked about a lot of things. He couldn't refuse this order, to do so would bring Rissling and his ghouls into his barracks looking for any infraction. If they did, and they would, they'd find Eva, he would sign all their death warrants on the spot.

The worst part was that he was absolutely stuck doing this terrible crime. If he refused, Rissling would twist it around and immediately make Klaus into the demon.

As Klaus continued his walk of death, he stopped at the sounds of hushed voices. They definitely were yelling, but doing it in as hushed of tones as they could.

A thin, gaunt boy was pinned beneath a heavier boy and was getting pummeled. The third boy stood apart from the two, his eyes constantly searching for danger, until he spotted Klaus. His face went pale and his eyes large. As Klaus took another step towards the boys on the ground a young Jewish man about 17 came running around the corner almost bumping into him. Klaus instantly grabbed the butt of his pistol, but relaxed his grip when the young Jew hold his hands up and stepped a few respectful steps backwards.

Klaus turned his attention back to the boys. The thin one would likely die anyway. The heavier one, if he survived the camp could be a worker. He would take the younger and smaller child, though both children likely wouldn't survive the camp or would simply be killed anyway.

The young Jewish man seemed to realize Klaus's thoughts. "I am Jules. The littler one is my brother. The other is a new prisoner." Klaus just shrugged. He already made up his mind, the Jew's statement inconsequential. So much so, Klaus barely paid any attention. He didn't change his mind once it was set. Or at least he usually didn't, he thought to himself remembering his change of mind with that silly kid in his barracks.

"Rissling came through a while ago, maybe about 10 minutes. He wants a piepel. He said he was coming for my brother one day. This one" the young Jew flung a hand up at the heavier boy, "believes that that is a good thing and has already broken my brother's nose for the 'honor'".

The young Jules spat at the ground in disgust and wiped his mouth with the back of his hand, on his sleeve and turned to face Klaus. "Spare my brother."

Klaus refused to look at the young Jules. If he took the other, heavier child, he would have done the bidding of a Jew. He might have gotten all mixed up when the Eva Jew giggled at him, but that was different. He was on edge in the crematory. It wasn't that he had felt weakness or pity for Eva…that girl, it was just he was on edge and had to make a quick decision. Klaus hated to make quick decisions. He liked time to think about things.

Jules saw that the guard's decision was made and knew what it meant. He slumped his shoulders, a few ragged breaths coming from deep inside him. He would not cry in front of this cruel bastard. He had failed and his brother would pay the price. Someway, he would find a way to kill them all. He would find a way out and a way to join the resistance. This ass would be the first to die.

Klaus walked to the struggling boys and picked both up by the back of their dirty striped uniforms. "Stoppen!" He ordered. He threw the bigger boy into the dirt and turned to walk away with the smaller child's arm still held tightly in his fist.

He watched as the heavier boy stood again, angrily. It was obvious he had come from a more gentile upbringing and Klaus stopped to watch him as the child stared arrogantly at him. The dumbass had no clue what he had been fighting for, just that it 'seemed' nice so he wanted to take it from the younger, smaller boy. The heavier boy acted as though he had never wanted for anything in his life, staring belligerently at Klaus as though *he* were the one in charge and not the other way around.

Klaus had, at one point, been the smaller boy. The arrogant stare of the heavier child bringing back memories of being bullied in their old neighborhood. He stood a moment longer and looked down at the child he was holding. The child stood silent, head down, knowing his fate. The older child stood watching, eyes flashing hatred at the younger boy. Klaus made another quick decision. He strode over, still with the smaller child's uniform bunched in his fist. He grabbed the older kid roughly and turned to face the young Jules. Klaus shoved the littler boy into his brother roughly. He began to drag the older kid away.

Klaus turned quickly at the sounds of running feet behind him. He turned to see the boy looking up at him. "It's my fault for speaking about it."

Klaus glared at the boy "You would die for the idiot that wanted to kill you?"

As the younger boy went to speak, his eyes full of pity Jules stepped to him and cuffed him upside the head. "Go! Get out of here and take your dumb friend with you, before you both cause more trouble!" Jules turned and met Klaus's eyes while the two younger boys ran off. "I wouldn't allow him to die. But I would die for him." He looked down and crossed his arms across his chest. "I would die for him. If you have to hunt for Rissling again, find me instead."

Klaus gave the slightest nod and left, the boy dragging along behind him willingly and looking to be full of self-importance. Knowing that the kid was about to die, Klaus hated the order he had been given, but he also hated people like this selfish idiot, even if he was nothing but a child, another job duty.

Once he had tossed the child into Rissling's barracks without a word he left to return to his own. He found himself sort of looking forward to going home after the experience he had. Even if he had to suffer the company of a tiny scrap of a Jew, it wasn't *that* bad. She provided entertainment, along with a million irritating questions. He guessed he tolerated her, nothing more. Reminding himself, as he did every day, that when he got too annoyed with her, he could simply kill her then. Sonja was a constant thought in his head as of late. He hadn't been able to save her, but he could, if he wanted to, save this creature and her big eyes.

The day hadn't been as terrible as he thought it would have been. Sure, a child was going to die, but he had inadvertently saved two more…three if you counted him not shooting Jules when he dared to speak to him after nearly crashing into him. He almost felt himself turning into a pansy as he walked.

He stood for a moment on his porch. He was glad he had spared Josef from that kind of a mission. Klaus was simply following orders nothing more. It's what he did. He was a soldier, one of the best. Josef was too, but he didn't have enough stomach and a bit too much heart.

He lit a cigarette, inhaling deeply as he looked over the portion of the camp he could see. Josef had to leave. He could take that dumb girl with him too. Klaus admitted to himself again that while he might be a bit fond of her, he sure as hell wouldn't die to save her. Josef's pansy ass would...and Klaus would die for his friend and brother.

The only alternative was to get Eva the hell out of here along with Josef. It was the only way. Josef, his closest friend needed to leave.

That too posed a problem. The Russians were rumored to be killing SS on sight. It would be just his stupid luck to get Josef out of here, just to have him get shot for a war criminal a mile from the gate. He had a lot of thinking to do.

Chapter 24

Hanna spent the last couple months hoping to die. She got even thinner by the day. She had no mirror in which to see herself, but she could feel how gaunt she was becoming. She raised a hand to her face, her fingers nearly sinking into her eye sockets. She knew she wouldn't last much longer, and that was ok. She was ready to go. It was time. She should have died with her child. She was the sole cause of her child's death. Her last remaining shred of sanity was saved by the knowledge that her child had died quickly.

Marta lay quietly thinking on their shared bunk. She didn't know what else she could do for her friend. "Hanna…when that nasty guard said that Eva was still alive, maybe he wasn't as cruel as I thought. Maybe he was telling the truth?"

Hanna rolled over slowly, weakly. Her dark eyes so full of pain, awaiting death a moment earlier now held the slightest light of hope in them. It wasn't that bright spark that had burned in her eyes when her child was alive, but where there was nothing but death in them a few seconds ago…there was something more now.

Marta hated herself. Part of her wanted to chastise herself for being so careless and cruel with her friends heart, but she felt she had had no other choice. She would do anything, anything at all to give her friend hope.

Marta had finished her time in the 'house', which was simply nothing more than a brothel. She was chosen simply because she was not a Jew, and she had a shade lighter hair than many of the women in the camp. She also realized that her so called talents and physical attributes had granted her slightly more favors than most of the other women. After all, she was only a gypsy; to the officers that were not nearly as terrible a crime as being a Jew was in this awful world they found themselves imprisoned in.

Hanna picked up the piece of bread that Marta had offered her and brought it to her lips. A small reward Marta had been given for her 'skills'. "Do you really think so Marta? Could that cruel bastard actually have saved my baby?"

Marta told the truth as she knew it…no more subterfuge on her part, "Oh sweet Hanna. I don't know, but what I do know is that he doesn't usually beat anyone. The ones who have been beaten by him have whispered that it was the best beating they have gotten. They said that the more they pretended to fall and wail, the less he actually struck them, no matter that he acted as though he were hitting them more. Few blows actually hurt."

Hanna chewed thoughtfully; barely aware she was even eating. Marta hid a smile. As long as she could keep Hanna thinking and talking, she might live. Marta handed Hanna a cup, and she drank distractedly. "If my baby, my dear Eva is still alive, she must be wondering if I am ok. I must go to her." As though in a trance, Hanna stood to walk to the barracks door.

Oh dear God, "No!" Marta yelled, as quietly as she could and still get Hanna's attention. Her desperate ploy to give her friend hope was threatening to unravel. "No you can't go to her. If Eva is alive, it has to be a secret. You will put her in danger if you go to her."

Carefully Hanna perched on the end of her bunk. Of course, Marta was right. Marta raised her eyes and gave a silent sigh of thanks. "Promise me Hanna, promise me you won't go there and endanger her if she is still alive? And, Hanna…please remember that it might have been just a cruel joke, but he might have been telling the truth. "

Hanna washed down her bread and nodded. Marta was right again. She lay back down in her bunk and smiled for the first time in months. What if her baby truly were still alive? Was that just too much of a farfetched hope to hold onto? Deep down, she knew Marta was just trying to placate her, to help her and get her to eat. Yet, some of the stuff she said *was* true. Josef actually wasn't nearly as much of a tyrant like many were.

Despite the odds being against her, Hanna found a new will to live. If by some inconceivable chance her child was alive, Hanna would live to be reunited with her again. If she truly was dead...Hanna would still live. She would live to tell the world her story. She had to live, even if it meant lying to herself every day.

Another long month in the camp passed. Hanna was becoming better by the day. She had filled out again, or at least as much as one could inside the camp. Marta had been able to take some extra food now and then from the kitchen when she was working. It was never enough, not near enough...but every morsel helped. She loved Hanna, and would do anything for her including risking her life for a few stale pieces of bread.

Occasionally the same guard crept in and dropped a few pieces of food onto the women's bunk. One morning they awoke to find two delicious but rather dry sandwiches. Both women quietly discussed how the sandwiches tasted burnt, although there was nothing burnt on the sandwiches. It was the day that Hanna should have been celebrating her daughters 6th birthday.

Marta was well past the two week deadline Heinrich had given and was showing enough that one could tell she was pregnant if she were not careful. The fact that she was so thin it was almost impossible didn't matter.

As much as was allowable, Marta stayed away from as many prying eyes as she could and tried to conceal her pregnancy with larger shirts and stooping a bit at the waist. It was rumored by a few men that the young soldier was the father. They talked as men do, but in the end, they knew a pregnant woman who was pulling on the heart strings of a young guard would have to be remedied. No matter how much Jonah tried to pretend he disliked the girl, it was noticeable the slightly extra care she had been given. She had to go. And soon. There was no question.

Chapter 25

Commander Rissling remained in camp. Through letter's he had been careful to relay to his commanding officers that having three camp commanders was benefiting the outfit. More barracks were being erected, more prisoners were arriving daily and of course, he told them, he didn't mind staying another few weeks.

While he hadn't been able to put his finger on it, he knew that somehow he had slowly been losing the respect of the men under his control. Sure the Jews and the other swine still ran as far from his reach as they could, but it was but a small victory. His men no longer treated him as though he were their commander any longer. His transfer papers had been in for some time, but he wasn't quite ready to go yet. There were several more things he wanted to do yet before he transferred out.

It bothered him that those new upstarts had killed Eva. Without her to constantly berate, he found himself with no one else to 'fight' with.

Most of the hardened men had begun to look at him with disgust. Rumors had started circulating around the camp regarding his behavior with some of the male prisoners. He knew Klaus and Josef had to be behind it. Surely no one knew what he actually did!

In the beginning, the inmates would grovel and plead and do all they could with hopes that THEY would be the one to catch his eye and escape. They had bowed down and attended to his every wish and command.

Nowadays, they didn't even bother to *try* to win his affection. The apathy they displayed angered Rissling. They no even longer bothered to try to appease him! That they were in such poor condition that they probably could not even try was beside the point. He could care less about that. The fact they didn't even try to please him irritated him to no end. Keeping his secret became harder and harder. As hard as his dick used to get with the crying and pleading used to be.

Now it barely even stood.

Klaus had been sent to find another child or a young man on the cusp of adulthood. The last piglet hadn't even been worth bothering with. It had been a disappointment. Perhaps Rissling needed a challenge again.

As Klaus wandered the barracks alley he came across the skinny kid and his brother from his last hunt.

Jules recognized the stare Klaus gave to him and said nothing. He turned instead to his kid brother and his brother's friend. "Say nothing to no one and stay out of everyone's way. Especially that Rissling monster. Keep out of his sight. Keep out of his way and say nothing to anyone."

The boy looked down and nodded. "You're leaving aren't you?" he spoke softly.

Jules knelt and held his brothers chin up to look at him. He moved his hand from his brother's chin to the side of his face.

"Yes. It is the way it will be. You stay quiet and out of the way. You got that? You remember everything I taught you?"

The kid nodded sadly again, a tear sliding from the corner of his eye to balance off the end of his nose reflected the bright sunshine. Jules wiped it off and pulled his brother tightly into their last embrace. He pulled his brothers friend into the hug and held them both for a moment until Klaus cleared his throat. "You boys remember everything I taught you, Ok?"

Jules quickly stood and nodded to Klaus. Both men turned and walked away without a backwards glance. The boys watched them: Jules young brother with tear-filled eyes. He wished he had been the one to die the last time Klaus came hunting. Then he would never know the pain of losing the last of his family. His brother along with his friend was the last ones. No one ever returned from being sent to Rissling.

The boy ran, his friend trailing behind to the farthest barracks. His tear streaked face noticed by several of the prisoners who slowly turned their backs. They would let the child grieve, unwatched. They alone understood his pain, and knew what the tears meant.

Rissling got up from his bed and looked over at the latest crud to hit his bed sheets. This one had been better than any of the others. His vacant eyes stared at the ceiling, appearing dead, probably wishing he was, Rissling smiled at the thought.

Rissling sat on the chair opposite the bed and looked back. This man had satisfied him decently, but not as others had so many years and partners ago. This one though, he had kept for three days, which was an uncommon thing. It was just that this young man, Jules had spirit and had fought back *just enough* and acquiesced just the same to keep intriguing Rissling.

Rissling had no idea the spirit displayed was nothing more than a survival game for the young man. He knew ultimately he would die, but hope that he might escape or live, kept him on high alert and in sync with the moods of Rissling.

Rissling prepared for his day, getting dressed and smiled for the first time in a while. This one had kept entertaining him. He had even fed the Jew, something he never did. He might keep this one a bit longer. He found the fight that was just perfect for him. Entertaining, but just exhausted enough to make sure he stayed safe. Yeah, he would keep him another day or so. He might even give him some more food, just to up his stamina a bit more, make him just a few degrees stronger. Then he would have some more fight in him, the more the better, but only to a certain extent, of course. All the better for Rissling, he felt safe and adding even the slightest hint of more danger excited him. He would let this Jew Pig recover and eat and then he would begin again, this time would be the Jews last time though.

Rissling smiled again as he walked out the door. "I'll come back. You won't like it, but I'll be back. Again and again for you." He shut and locked his door outside and smiled again, perfecting his predatory grin. Let the refuse in there think he would be saved. See if he still got the same performance!

Rissling stood outside his door and pondered his decision. He felt a nagging feeling that he should dispose of his latest garbage quickly. He didn't have anything on his schedule that couldn't wait a while longer. He turned back and unlocked the door. He would judge the next performance by his prisoner and then kill him. He smiled once more. His appointments could wait. He had work to do.

Chapter 26

"They know about us Hanna. All those people in the village right there know what's going on! How could they not! Why don't they help us, Hanna?"

Hanna sighed and pulled her friends head to her own shoulder, "You cannot blame them Marta. They would end up in here. If they pretend not to see, they will live." Hanna and Marta had both heard of the rumors of the fence lines being direct escape routes to freedom in the village. Yet, no miraculous daring escapes had happened that the women knew of. Neither one of the women dared to talk to anyone else about the villagers.

Hanna had been told by an old man not to trust anyone. That anyone could turn on you, for anything.

Marta sniffled and rubbed her face with the dirty sleeve of her uniform shirt and nestle her head under Hanna's chin. "It's so awful. They are right across the fence, living! We are in here slowly dying. I hate them. I would kill them myself if I could."

Hanna stroked her friend's hair, once so vibrant and now so thin and like straw to the touch. It had also lightened from all the hours in the sun.

"No, Marta, you can't let that kind of hate into your heart, into your womb. Your baby, Marta, think of your baby. If I were on that other side of the fence, I might do the same thing they are in order to protect Eva. You might do the same to protect your small and growing flower."

Marta abruptly sat up. The closeness the two women had, now just a memory; a warm spot upon Hanna's shoulder, quickly cooling off.

Marta glared at Hanna, angrier then Hanna had ever seen her before, "Would you Hanna? Would you look at us in here behind this wall of death and walk away? How could you, Hanna! I wouldn't." Marta screamed, her voice echoing inside of the barracks.

Hanna reached up and pulled her friends arm, entreating her to sit. She patted the bunk next to her. As Marta sat, Hanna wrapped her arms around her friend and spoke quietly, hoping to calm her friend before any of the guards came to see what the yelling was about.

"I'm not saying it is the right action. But who will they tell? What do they say? Then what? Your family is killed? Do you save strangers or your family, Marta? It's wrong. It's right. I pity them too, I would hope that their hearts hurt when the fall asleep at night. They, warm and cozy in their beds, knowing that we are dying cold and alone in here." Hanna's voice broke and Marta squeezed her arm.

Marta looked down and pulled at the loose thread on her sleeve. A large tear rolled down her face, streaking her dirty face with a single clean spot.

Both women embraced a moment longer before facing the day ahead of them. They hugged again as they left their bunks; the life and death they faced every day. Neither knowing if they would ever see each other alive again.

No one would ever know exactly, even Rissling, but for some reason he rose once more out of his bed this day and in a completely uncharacteristic move, strode to the bed and looked down. "Use the shower. Eat this food here and don't leave this room." Rissling would try a different tactic, much like the tactics he had used in the beginning. This one had actually been a bit sporting. Rissling was not tired of him yet, although everything in Rissling was screaming to get rid of this play toy lest he be discovered.

The man on the bed closed his eyes, one single tear escaping. He knew about the deaths of the other countless men who had been through these doors. He knew none had stayed as long as he and they had all been murdered. He would be too. The only bright spot was the fact that he was clean and had been fed for the last couple days. Today he would find a way to escape, or die. Even three days of food wasn't worth his life. Today he would die...or Rissling would, which of course meant he would too. Sometimes a man stood and fought, and died fighting. Today Jules would die. He would die on his feet, and Rissling was coming with him.

The depths to which he felt he had sunk astounded him. In his prime had he ever been propositioned he would have either killed the man propositioning or he would have made him very sorry. In his weakened state, the fact that he hadn't been killed, and the pity bestowed upon him from his enemy was too much to bear. If Rissling knew the single tear was not from gratitude but from a hate more than he could ever imagine, Rissling would have killed his prisoner without a second glance- just like he usually did. Rissling had no idea the dangerous game he was playing with the young Jules.

Rissling strode from his barracks and locked the door behind him again. His windows had been nailed shut on both sides a long time ago.

He was not in a pleasant mood. His whipping child was gone; her broken shell of a mother didn't bother to cower before him any longer. Her apathy seemed to enrage him, but it wasn't even any sport to hit her. It was as though she never noticed.

Rissling walked the courtyard and watched Jonah, the young Lieutenant and constant companion of Heinrich, walking out of his barrack. He had a spring in his step and laughed as he walked out. He turned to lock his door and stopped when he noticed Rissling looking at him. The young Lt had been a constant irritant of Rissling's. Of all the guards, only the young one, who was constantly under the wing of the more seasoned guards...almost as though they were protecting him?

"You! Why are you just leaving your barracks? Who's covering for you today?" Rissling yelled to the young Lt.

The young man, Jonah, stood on his porch step forgetting to lock the door, leaving the key in the knob. He quickly scanned the area and saw the new Commanders and his old ally and friend walking down the row. He wasn't sure what was wrong with the commander but something wasn't right. His eyes seemed both interested and yet vacant at the same time if such a thing could be described. Jonah felt a tightening in his gut. Heinrich had told him many times to never ignore his gut. His gut would always warn him.

He stalled for a moment at the door before slowly walking down the steps. Jonah hoped Heinrich and the two new commanders would notice something seem awry and hurry. Even if they didn't, at least he could stall until they got closer. He faced the commander in the dirt alley before saying anything. "I'm on afternoon watch. I've every right to be here this morning, same as you." Once Jonah was closer to Rissling, he could see clearly, the man seemed off. His eyes, that normally were sharp as a hawk seemed to peer right through him, as though Jonah were merely an illusion. Chill bumps raced up Jonah's arms and settled in the back of his head, where he felt his hair stand on end. Something was definitely not right with this guy. Jonah watched as Heinrich, Josef and Klaus just lazily strolled along.

Rissling became annoyed this upstart didn't put his full attention on him. Rissling was still the Commander and that position required all respect.

Rissling walked toward the young Jonah, his fists balled tightly. This kid was always protected by the older officers and he was not having it today, even if that damned mustached Heinrich was close to him. He was not letting this dumb kid get away with speaking to him in that tone.

Perhaps if his inmate had groveled and begged for his life, this day would have turned out differently. Maybe if it hadn't stuck in his head how he had let a prisoner live this day. He felt good about his decision when he left his barracks, but as the minutes wore on, he felt less sure about his decision. It was just a nagging thought at first, but the more he thought about it, the more he felt he had been made a fool of. He had been sure that the pain he had inflicted...

Well, it was of no consequence now. He would simply yell at this uppity young Lt and then head back to kill the Jew. Or maybe sport with him again. Rissling wasn't sure which and that made him angry. He rather enjoyed sporting with this one. But no problem, he would just kill him and the odd feeling would go away.

Rissling walked until he was face to face with the young Lt and let fly with his fist. He connected solidly to the young man's face. To his surprise the young man barely staggered backwards before straightening back up... Startled, the young man stood for only a moment before throwing the punch right back. Rissling was blindsided when the kid came back swinging. He was not used to fighting with anyone that wasn't more than half starved and had all their strength.

Heinrich saw the kid getting ready to throw a punch and tried to yell out a warning. Rissling was probably one of the worst people the kid could hit. No matter what, one did not hit the commanding officer. The kid let fly before a sound even came from Heinrich's mouth.

Rissling was used to dishing out whatever punishments he saw fit or that tickled his fancy, but he was not used to being on the defensive side. The punch from Jonah connected hard on his jaw and Rissling was sent falling backwards and sliding in the dirt. Jonah stood and watched as Rissling sat in the dirt, his uniform already dusty and his face red.

His pistol fell from its holster; Rissling had forgotten to close the flap as he had left his barracks.

Klaus and Josef along with Heinrich ran toward Rissling and the Lt They had seen Rissling throw the first punch, and when Jonah landed his.

Rissling rolled over on his stomach and saw his pistol in front of him. He looked at his pistol for a few split seconds and then grabbed it.

Jonah was already walking back to his barrack door to secure it and head out, away from this fool. Rissling quickly stood; his gun hanging silently in his hands. As he brought the gun up to aim at the young Lt a woman's scream rang out. The Lt looked up towards his door and then turned around to face Rissling.

"You're going to pay for that you little shit!" Rissling wiped the blood from his mouth with the back of his left hand, his right hand holding his pistol aimed level at Jonah's chest.

Josef, Klaus and Heinrich grabbed their pistols and ran toward Rissling and Lt They ran hard, even though they knew they were still too far away.

Heinrich yelled as he ran, "Rissling, stand down." Trying to diffuse the situation. That kid meant a lot to him!

Jonah watched as Rissling's index finger moved onto the trigger and knew he was going to be killed. His eyes opened wide just as another shrill scream sounded through the courtyard. Marta leapt through the now open door and lunged in front of Jonah just as the gun fired.

Jonah grabbed Marta's thin waist and felt the bump of their child between them as he felt the hot blood from her chest leaking onto his uniform. His face went pale as he looked down into her face.

Marta looked up and him and whispered. "I couldn't tell you before. You know I loved you, Jonah." Jonah looked at her some more and back at Rissling. He slowly knelt onto the porch boards, wanting to answer her questioning eyes, but knowing the shots would bring in other guards. He looked once more into her beautiful face and once more over at Rissling and then Heinrich who was just about to the porch steps.

Marta closed her eyes and softly whimpered in pain. Jonah felt the tears on his cheeks before he even knew he was crying. He slowly sank to his knees until he held her head in his lap and bent down over her. Only a few months ago he was bent over taking her beautiful lips under his own. At first it, or rather she, had been only a conquest; a rousing night of drinking and gambling. She had just been a winning poker bet and good for some laughs from the other guards.

As the months had passed she had slowly become more. He didn't know when that happened, but he sure knew now that it had. As her life's blood spilled through the cracks on his old porch and down on his thighs as he held her, he realized that she, and their child had meant more to him than he ever could have imagined.

Heinrich ran to his side, just as Marta opened her eyes again. He could see the pain in her eyes and Heinrich had seen how she had thrown herself in front of his young comrade. A woman like Marta, even if she was a mere gypsy was worth her weight in gold, and now she would be gone. He met her eyes and nodded at her. It was but a simple gesture of great respect from one free man... to a now free woman.

He knelt with Jonah and laid a hand on his back. As other officers began to amass, he looked around to Josef and Klaus who began to shoo them away. This was not a circus tent, and he didn't want all these people looking at his young friend.

"Marta, I know it seemed like I didn't, but I loved you too. My sweet, brave woman... I would have married you. I would have-" Jonah's voice cracked and broke as he began sobbing, tightly holding on to the woman who had saved his life.

She slowly lifted her hand to his face, death making her hand shake weakly "I would have been proud to call you my husband" She winced in pain and closed her eyes. "My Jonah" she whispered his name on her last breath and closed her beautiful brown eyes. She shuddered only slightly as her spirit left. Jonah looked to Heinrich. "Please don't bury her in the graves. Find a place for her, Heinrich ? You'll do that?" Heinrich nodded slightly. "We will, Jonah, we will."

Jonah ran his hand over the small bump that housed his child and felt the small stirrings beneath his hands. The weak movements feeling like a small whisper of wind blowing past his hands. He realized then that that's exactly what it was. The stirring beneath his hand kicked a couple more times and was silent. The hidden life Marta had called a butterfly was gone; along with the woman he realized he belatedly realized he loved and who had given her life to protect him.

Jonah looked into Heinrich's face again. "That could have been my family."

Heinrich took a deep breath, for what may have been the first time in this hell he found himself in, thought about his life and his direct orders so far. He looked into the eyes of the young man who had become like the son he had never had. He spoke from his heart; he spoke as a father and grandfather, not as an officer of the most hated regime that mankind would ever know, "Son that was your family. I'm sorry Jonah."

Chapter 27

Jonah stood and looked at Rissling. He never said a word, just slid his pistol slowly out of its holster as he stepped off the porch, Marta's blood covering his chest. Heinrich leapt out of way, lest Rissling shoot him but still he shoved Jonah away as well, trying to save his young friend. Rissling never flinched. He lifted his pistol and shot.

Jonah felt a hot searing near his right eye as he felt the weakness overcome him. He fell into Heinrich's arms who slowly knelt with him. Jonah couldn't form any words but his eyes kept trying to find Marta, even though he was no longer able to turn his head. Heinrich drug him backwards the couple paces to Marta. Jonah turned his head to look at her face and a ghost of a smile appeared on his face. He reached to hold her hand, but death took him before he could finish entwining her fingers with his.

Heinrich reached over and closed his eyes, while at the same time, closing the young man's fingers around the fingers of the girl he had loved, and who had given her life to love him.

"What in the hell was that, Rissling!!" Klaus ran to Rissling and pulled the gun out of his hand.

"You saw him! He pulled a gun on me!" Rissling yelled his voice high pitched in his panic.

Heinrich stood, "Rissling killed them both, Sir" He walked towards Klaus and Rissling until he stood in front of them. "I liked that kid." Were the only words he said as he pulled back and punched Rissling for the second time that day. Rissling fell, and both men watched him fall, neither lifting a hand to help him. Rissling stood shakily, blood dripping off his chin. Both punches that had hit his face sent his cheek into his teeth. He spit out the fresh blood and wiped his chin with his sleeve.

"Sir, I need to pick a crew to help me. And I need one of the women too. I'm sending Jonah back to his home, and I'm sending Marta with him." His tone brooked no argument, his eyes flashed toward Rissling, daring him to defy him. "I need one of the women to go into the storage and pull out a dress."

Klaus nodded. He hadn't heard what anyone had said previously, but he and he alone had watched as Mustache clasped the young lovers' hands together.

Heinrich ran to his now assembled men. He spied Hanna sobbing on the outskirts of the field. Despite the care he had just given his fallen and murdered comrade, he didn't spare much of a thought for Marta's friend. He informed his men to bring Jonah to the camp clinic. There he would begin the preparations to send his young friend…and the mother of his child home with him. He pointed toward Hanna and Josef nodded.

"Hanna!" Josef barked the order. "Follow me"

Hanna walked slowly past the body of her only friend. She followed behind the man who had murdered her child. She had no choice. She almost envied Marta. Marta was no longer a prisoner. Marta was free.

Hanna looked at her fallen friend and stifled another sob and stumbled behind Klaus and Josef. They marched directly to their barracks. At the door Josef cleared his throat and jiggled the door knob. Had Hanna been just a bit more aware, less shocked at the loss of her dear friend, she would have heard the slight thump inside the house, the small feet running. Klaus cleared his throat loudly at the noise and walked into the barracks behind Josef and motioned for Hanna to follow.

The barracks were surprisingly clean and Hanna was surprised. Josef motioned toward the table and Hanna sat. She wasn't sure what she was going to be doing but so far she seemed safe. She sat, tightly, stiffly not sure of herself. Klaus stood, looking down at her and Josef sat in the chair opposite from her. Briefly, Hanna wondered at the addition of a third chair to the barracks sole table.

"You knew about Marta and Jonah?" Klaus spoke.

Hanna sighed, knowing that her involvement or at least knowledge of the affair would come out sooner or later.

"I knew of it." Hanna slowly said her eyes still downcast staring at the table. Josef grunted, he thought as much. It had been rumored for some time in the main barracks commons. "Hanna, go to the storage. I need a dress suitable for a lady; a good, classy lady. Get another woman to help you bring the body to the crematorium. While there, Heinrich will come to you. You will garb her in the best dress you can find. We will send her home with Jonah." He paused for a second, turned back to Hanna, "Pick one to show their child."

Klaus grabbed her arm firmly as she turned in her chair, preparing to leave to complete their requests, "Find a ring as well. Tell no one, or you die." Klaus ordered.

Hanna looked first into Josef's face and then back to Klaus. These men were actually showing decency? These child murderers cared enough...that Marta was going to be buried in a real cemetery? Hanna choked back another sob as Josef knelt down.

Klaus cleared his throat and stepped away from the table, striding over to look out the window. Josef spoke in the silence of the room. "Hanna, everything will be ok. All is not lost."

Hanna felt the anger building inside her and didn't trust herself to look at that man again. Her daughter was dead, now her best friend and confidante was dead too ...and this pompous ass was telling her that everything would be ok? It was not Ok. It would never again be ok.

Of course everything was ok for him. Those Nazi pigs had ruined her entire life and then told her it was ok. God, why didn't they just kill her and end her torment? Why was she made to suffer so much, for nothing more than being born?

Josef saw the shaking of her slight body and hoped that he'd been able to help her. He had no idea she was shaking with suppressed rage, instead of the sorrow he thought she had been shaking from. She sure was full of sorrow, but hate had slowly begun to overtake her pain.

He turned to Klaus and nodded. The men headed for the door. "You get that done right now, Hanna. We're headed to the commander's office."

Chapter 28

Rissling stood and watched the flurry of activity around him. What had come over him, he simply didn't know. Now that it was over, he wanted to leave. Perhaps the stress of "his job" got to him. Whatever it was, he was going back to his barracks and they would find him and talk to him there. In his private quarters; when *he* was ready for them

Rissling walked to his porch and unlocked his door. He looked both ways to find no one was immediately following him, although several prisoners and guards were watching him from afar. He paused for a second before entering his room. He knew he was leaving this place today. He would pack his bags and just leave.

He looked up to find the young man he had left in his bed sitting on the edge of the bed. The young man looked up with red rimmed eyes. Rissling almost felt as though he wanted to comfort him, or at least sport with this worthy toy one more time, but he knew now that he had to get rid of his latest play thing since the other soldiers would be here shortly. In fact, this latest plaything was probably the cause of all of this! He had to be! It was his fault and now he would die!

He pulled his knife from its sheath on his hip and aimed it at towards the young man. "Down on your knees." Rissling reached around behind him and began closing the door. As the door clicked behind him he felt a draft of air as though someone was moving behind him.

Rissling spun around to find the single drab curtain blowing in the open window. Before he could spin around back to his prisoner he felt the wire cutting into his neck.

His hands struggled to pull the wire away, already dropping the knife within seconds, but the wire only seemed to get tighter with every attempt.

"Sterben Nazi Schwein" the hoarse voice grunted into his ear. He wasn't sure if he was actually hearing footsteps on his porch or not, and for a brief moment was happy to see Heinrich walk in. His Jewish assailant had not yet noticed the new figure in the room.

Heinrich looked over the scene. The half-dressed young Jewish man with freshly washed hair and body covered in fresh bruises. His eyes took in the messed up bed, the bloodstains on the mattress and the newly removed nail from the windowsill to open the window. He took in the entire scene for a moment while Rissling gasped and thrashed. Finally, he turned his eyes to the terrified gasping face of Rissling. Heinrich watched for another second until the Jewish man noticed him standing there. Heinrich met his eyes, stood for a full couple of seconds more as the young Jew pulled the wire even tighter without leaving the gaze of Heinrich. Heinrich met Rissling's terrified eyes once more briefly then closed the door quietly; sealing the fate of Rissling inside.

A few minutes later when Rissling ceased to move, the Jewish man climbed out the back window of the barracks and knelt below the window. He felt the bile rise into his throat, but he couldn't let that happen. He swallowed hard a couple times to keep it down.

He was on high alert looking and listening, his heart pounding nearly out of his chest. He wasn't sure what had happened or why the officer had let him continue. When they had met eyes, he knew he was dead. Yet, here he was- absolutely alive and for the most part, doing well. The officer simply closed the door and left Rissling to him. He couldn't believe this turn of events. He was clean for the first time in months, he had food in his belly and he was so close to the gate. He could almost escape...but he had his brother to think about and he wasn't free yet.

A noise to the right had him jumping to his feet. Heinrich stood with a rifle trained at the chest of the man who had killed the camp commander. Heinrich spoke quietly. "He killed Jonah." Years later, he would wonder why he ever bothered to inform the Jew.

Heinrich lowered the gun and held up one finger, signaling the Jew to wait. The young Jules nodded, he would wait. Running after the Nazi told him to wait would be nothing more than suicide. Standing here waiting for the Nazi who had just watched him kill an officer was suicide as well. Yet he stood, waiting… hopefully for his life.

Heinrich disappeared behind the building. A few thumps inside the recently vacated Commanders building and all was silent. Jules stood quietly, back pressed against the building carefully watching his surroundings, expecting a trap be sprung at any moment.

Heinrich appeared again and walked to the Jew. He thrust a shirt and pants at him "Wear these and walk right out from the corner of the guard tower. I'll call the alarm in two minutes for Rissling. All eyes will be here. Run at the alarm. Jonah was my friend. I would have killed you. I still can. And know that someone will die in your place. "

There was no mention of Marta, nor would there ever be again. She was gone, and it mattered not.

"You have two minutes and I might change my mind before then. I wouldn't waste a second."

The Jew opened his mouth to thank Heinrich but thought better of it. Heinrich turned around to walk away. A whisper of a prayer filled the soot filled air, "Gott rette diesen Mann und begrüße seinen jungen Freund."

Heinrich turned one last time, to look at the Jew. The young Jew had asked God to save him and to welcome his young friend, Jonah . Heinrich met the young man's eyes, seeing for perhaps the first time, the humanity in them. The young man had asked God to save *him*. He hadn't thanked god for his escape, he asked God to protect *him*, his captor. The man asked his God to welcom Jonah into his kingdom. Heinrich spoke around the odd and rather unusual catch in his throat.

"Two minutes. Go!" and he walked away. He would never know if the man made it once he got through the gates. As an old man, Heinrich would wonder now and then if the man had survived.

The young man would quietly walk out of Majdanek and recover from his injuries and would go on to save many lives. He would never forget the one man, the Nazi, that was faced with duty or honor…and he chose honor and thus saved the life of hundreds of people.

It would be Heinrich's punishment, in his twilight years, that he would never know of the good that he had done in that one day. He would die an old man, alone with only his memories and awaiting his judgement day. Jonah and Marta would lay forever, their child between them. Jules would have but one son, and he would name him Jonah, in honor of the young man who loved a woman. For a young man who was loved so as a surrogate son. A young man so loved, that his death had given him freedom and his life. Jules was no dummy; he knew that had it been under any other circumstances than his young friend being killed by Rissling that he would have died that day. He owed his life to a young man he had only ever seen from a distance. Jonah's shocking death by one of his own countrymen, had secured his freedom.

Chapter 29

As the alarm sounded, Heinrich heard the running feet heading his way. Josef and Klaus ran onto the porch. "What happened?"

"Came back and found him like that." Heinrich flatly stated and then lit a cigarette.

Josef and Klaus met eyes; they too had seen the messed up bed, the slight bloodstains and the discarded dirty prisoner's uniform next to the bed. Rumors were not above them, and many had said that Rissling had another side to him. Josef took a step inside the barracks taking stock of the room. "Did you move anything in here?"

Heinrich took a deep drag off his cigarette, "No. Came here to talk to him and found him just like this."

Klaus stepped inside the room and knelt at the body of Rissling. "He's been strangled to death. Let me see your hands." He ordered Heinrich.

Heinrich calmly held out his hands for both officers to see. It was plain to both of them that Heinrich was not the one to blame. His calm demeanor and lack of eye contact had them believing he knew more than he let on though.

Josef stood up from where he had knelt by the body. "Heinrich, what do think happened here?"

Heinrich was silent, and looked over the prone body of his former commanding officer. He waited another second before speaking, giving the young Jewish man an extra few seconds. Josef caught the quick look Heinrich shot towards the open window behind the bed. "Heinrich, did this man commit suicide after he shot Jonah?"

Heinrich pulled on his whiskers. "Yeah, I believe he did." He knew he needed all in agreement for this to work. "Klaus, you believe he just snapped out there and then came back here and killed himself?"

Klaus entered the room and closed the door behind him. He looked first at Josef and then to Heinrich. "No. I don't think he did, and no one else will either. But…." Klaus paused a moment and surveyed the room again quickly, meeting Heinrich's stare "I bet the wire snapped when he was over there by the bed and he rolled… here." Klaus met Heinrich's eyes and he raised his eyebrow… both men bent to move the body several inches closer to the beam in the middle of the room. "Now I bet he killed himself, don't you think?"

The three men looked down at Rissling for the last time. None removed their hats. Rissling to all of them had been almost a symbol of the Nazi depravity. He had reveled in anything evil. They had all done their jobs, but not with the excitement Rissling had. Heinrich met both the men's eyes and nodded. It was done. Klaus and Josef were in command now.

Josef and Klaus walked to the door while Heinrich kicked the uniform shirt farther under the bed. All three stepped out into the sunlight.

Their announcement was simple. "Rissling is dead. He has killed himself after he killed Jonah. Ship him home."
All three men stepped from the platform and walked away from the stunned crowd of Guards and the few brave prisoners watching.

Had any of the guards been listening, they would have heard a small whisper of a young boy to his friend, "Jules has escaped hasn't he?"

The other young boy nodded and smiled a gentle, but sad smile. "My brother lives. He will come back for me. I know he will. He has too!" The young boy would be the first of many saved by the young Jew Jules that Heinrich had let walk free from Majdanek.

Back in their barracks Josef and Klaus walked in through the door. Klaus shut it and leaned back against the door. "What the hell happened in there?"

Josef sat at their table and hit the toe of his boot against the table leg three times as he sat in silence.

A slight whisper of a sound and a small scraping noise, then Eva was at his knee. Josef gathered the small girl in his arms and tucked her head beneath his chin. "Dammit Klaus, I don't know. Heinrich knows something. Do you want to question him again?"

Klaus strode to the sink, pulling one of Eva's crooked pig tails on the way past. She reached up quickly and pulled her short pigtail out of his hands and made a face at him. He made a face back at her behind Josef's back. He filled up a cup with water, before turning around to lean on the sink and answer Josef.

"Yeah. But to find out what happened with Jonah. I could care less about Rissling. He's dead and I'm glad we're rid of him."

Josef gave Eva a squeeze, "Go now. We're going to have company." Eva hopped down and ran to Klaus, still leaned on the kitchen sink. One small shoe stomped on Klaus's foot and ground down on it. A giggle sounded in the gloom of the barracks and Eva was running for her hiding spot.

"Damn stray kittens running around all over in here. I'm going to have to clean house!" Josef laughed at his friend brusque manner, knowing Eva was smiling in her hiding spot.

Klaus took another drink of water, turned the spigot off and got the slight grin off his face before he turned back to face Josef.

"Get Heinrich in here. Let's settle this."

Chapter 30

"General, Sir, we're getting interference here. Might want to come and take a listen." The General rubbed the top of his nose, sighed and headed to the radio. Nonstop radio chatter, with usually little to no intelligence information had been coming across constantly. "What do you got?"

"It's in German. I'm not sure of all the words." The young private jumped from his seat at the command to let the General sit and listen.

"No shit, it's in German. You are in Germany", the General thought to himself. It wasn't that he didn't necessarily want to say it out loud, but these boys and men he was in charge of had a difficult time ahead of them.

According to several reports he had received there were some kind of work camps, some even called them death camps being run by the Germans. Reports had information about the worst kind of living hell anyone could even imagine. Sights so depraved, so horrific, that a man would never be the same after just witnessing it, let alone what he and his boys were to do. Walk into one and free the people. So far, it just sounded like a science fiction novel. People just didn't enslave millions of people and just kill them like the old slaughterhouse at home. It just didn't happen.

He did read the reports coming in, though. Apparently, some Jewish people had been escaping these extermination camps and rail-way freight cars and telling people what was happening. It seemed as though the rumors were true, but yet fighting against an evil of this magnitude had his men on high alert. If these evil folks could so casually throw away and murder their own brethren, what would they do to his boys?

No one believed it though, or at least they tried not to. Surely, it was all just propaganda put on by different governments to incite war. No one would take millions of people and murder them with no one in the surrounding towns saying anything about it. That didn't really happen, did it? Sure, they had happened across a few emaciated people along their way, but they just figured they had some disease and made sure to steer clear of them.

Mainly all they had seen were hordes of German soldiers, fighting against the allies who were there to clean up this mess that they had made.

It was just like the states to engage his boys in another war that they had no reason to get involved in. Well, there was a damn good reason so many men lined up to fight, the Japanese had killed many innocent lives at Pearl Harbor a couple years ago. Why weren't they just over there killing japs instead of being in Germany?

Just in case those horrific stories were real, the General of this unit was here for one reason, and one reason only- to see *his* boys through this damn fool war and come out the other side. If they were going to be freeing folks from a death camp, whatever that was, he wanted to make sure his boys went in as healthy and as happy as they could before evil took its spot in their hearts and minds.

Why were they cooling their heels in some damn Russian controlled town close to Poland for Christ sakes? The Russians were on the north end of Poland. Some of the shit he heard about the Russian soldiers didn't make him feel any better.

They were going to end up flanked on every side. What in the hell were they even doing there?

The General put on the headset. He grimaced as he always grimaced. He personally hated putting on a headset that was on someone else's head. He held the left ear piece up closer….and looked quickly around the room as he heard the incoming message.

"He is a traitor. I am his Commander. He has kidnapped a Jewish piglet from Majdanek and plans to escape with it in just a few days' time!"

The General's eyes went wide, and he gestured wildly to his interpreter, who wasn't there? Where the hell did that kid go now? He had to get this Nazi talking and find out more. But how were they going to do that? He cleared his throat as his Lt sat down beside him. He handed the other set of headphones over absently, until he realized the Lt. was not the constantly missing interpreter.

The other men gathered around pressing close to hear more. The general shrugged them off, pushing them backwards with an outstretched arm. "Bertrain, where the hell is Bert? Somebody get that damn kid."

While they waited for the interpreter to arrive, the young Lt spoke into the headphones, "Soldat wiederholen!" The General lifted his eyes to the young Lt Shyly, the young man pulled a small translation book out of his back pocket. "My mom thought it might come in handy, if I ran into any Germans." The General knew he should damn well give his young Lt hell for going ahead and acting on his own without a direct order. He decided though, to keep quiet until he found out how his young Lt had affected his communication with the German voice.

The voice came through loud and clear again. "Warte ab? Ich werde nicht warten . Holen Sie sich Ihre Scheiße zusammen!"

From behind the Commander, the always missing Bertrain appeared and began laughing. He pushed his sandy blond hair back from his forehead and laughed again. "He's giving you information and you told him to wait?"

"Where the hell were you this time?" The General bellowed, turning to watch the Bertrain kid take his spot at the radio.

"I was taking a shit. I didn't know someone was going to come up right then." The young Bertrain answered calmly. The kid never got bent out of shape over anything. Everything just seemed to fly right past him. Kid was without a worry in the world.

"Bertrain, you're always taking a shit. That's why you're nothing but skin and bones" the young Lt laughed and handed the headset to Bertrain.

The General shook his head, it never failed, that damn kid was always off doing something, when he was needed the most, and yet somehow everything always worked out perfect for him. Kid was like a lucky charm. No one knew where Bertrain came from, except from somewhere in Ky. He never spoke of his family, his life or anything, but that kid could speak like six different languages fluently, and here he was translating German in the damn army.

Bertrain sat down and looked at the commander, "Well Chief, let's find out what's going on, shall we?" The General just nodded and chuckled. "Go for it." Damn kid, he thought to himself, chuckling inward as he cringed again, "Sure hope that damn kid washed his hands!" he thought.

"Soldat! Lassen Sie Ihre Daten jetzt!" Bertain, looked around and laughed. "I told him to give me his information now." The men looked back and forth at each other, uneasy at the young man's tone to the voice on the other end of the line.

Bertain looked up at them and rolled his eyes, "I heard General in there, although he didn't give his rank. I outrank him. I am the United States. I ordered him to give me his information."

"How in the hell did you hear him on the shitter, Bert?" the young Lt asked.

The radio buzzed again... "I'm giving you information. You don't need to know anymore. A general has kidnapped a Jewish prisoner. He will be meeting another prisoner at a small pond just a few kilometers from Lublin."
"Give me a landmark and a day!"

"Give me your word the man will live!" The scratchy German voice crackled again Bertain raised an eyebrow at his General. The General scratched his nose, and looked around. All his men were looking at him, many shaking their heads. He could not guarantee a German soldiers life!

"Why should he live? What is his plan for the child?"

"That's not what I asked American pig!"

Bertrain looked back at his General. "Probably best we say he lives, and get the coordinates." Bertrain paused, "I would save a child, even if the world was crashing down around me."

The General looked down at his mysterious translator. In all the months they had been together, the kid was never serious. This was a new side of him

■■

"No! No guarantees!" A young soldier yelled, near the General's ear.

"Hey, Grayson! My ear is only 6 inches from your big mouth!" an older soldier barked back.

The General stuck a pinky finger in his ear and rubbed it around a bit. "Tell him you have my word. The man will live." Bertrain gave a quick nod and returned to the radio. "The man will live. You have the word of our General."

The radio was silent for a very long time. Minutes passed as the soldiers stood by waiting. A few turned to leave and the voice came back, stopping them.

Bertrain scribbled furiously as the name listed landmarks and coordinates. He turned to the General as the arrogant German voice ended their conversation.

He says there is a river that runs south out of Lublin. That there is a camp called Maj-Nek or something just south east of Lublin, but that river will flow due south.

The older soldier grabbed a map and placed it on the table, rolling it out quickly.

"That's 150 miles away!" The older soldier yelled towards the General, "We can't roll 150 miles north towards a death camp with only the word of some German fool! We don't even know if what he says is true! It's a damn trap!"

"We'll be there boys. This is what we came to do."

"To put us all in danger for the life of maybe one child?"

"A life is a life, boys. We've got three days to get there and back. I'm going, and I'm only taking volunteers. In three days, we're moving back south to the Alps and out of this damn place. Bertrain, I assume you can give a good reason as to why our radios aren't working?"

• •

"Yee-upp" Bertrain drawled, "I got it. I'm in. Let's go."
The General looked over his men. "Stay or go, the choice is yours, men. "

Eight of his men came with him; the remaining would wait for their return...if they returned.

■■

Chapter 31

The Villagers crawled slowly to the fence. Slowly over the last few weeks they had been cutting some of the wire on the bottom rows of wire. With the blacksmith's trade a readily accessible commodity, they had been able to stake the wires at each end before they cut between the stakes.

If you didn't know to look for the cut wires and the stakes holding them up to only look proper you never would know. Certainly, none of the 'wise' guards had caught on. Or at least it didn't seem they did. Tonight was the night they were going to pull the largest amount of prisoners out from under the fence, out of hell. Even if they could only save a couple, they would. They had to.

Dorek lay between the two fences. Someone was out there; he just couldn't tell if it was a prisoner or a German guard. He could feel the eyes on him. He lay silent beneath the black cloth they used to hide from the Germans. He uncovered just an eye to look back to Henryck. Henryck too, had just an eye sticking out from under the cloth.

Dorek looked to Henryck to see if there was any advice or direction in them. Asking the blacksmith silently what he should do. He watched as the Blacksmiths eyes went wide and slowly turned his head to face the other direction. Before he could even look all the way, strong arms gripped an arm of his and pulled him into the confines of the camp. As he went to scream, a strong hand slapped him hard across the face. He could feel the blood welling up from his mouth and down the front of his chin.

He looked up into the face of the angriest looking human he had ever seen. The steel grey eyes steady on his scared eyes. He choked back a sob and tried to wrench away from the iron grip of his captor.

The grip was relentless and Dorek knew this would be that day that he would die or be thrust into the most unimaginable horror. Either way he was dead, just one would be a bit faster than that of the other.

"You have one single chance to live. I know who you are, and I know what you have been doing." The Nazi pulled Dorek up to his face and yelled some more, "I order you to do one single task for me. You do it correctly and you live. You do it wrong and your whole village will be destroyed. You first. You got that?"

Dorek swallowed hard and bit back the pain in his collar bone where the Nazi was gripping. The iron grip never lessened as the Nazi talked.

Twice the Nazi made him repeat exactly what he had been told. When the Nazi seemed to think Dorek had done a good enough job of repeating him, he let go the grip on Dorek's shoulders.

The fist connected hard, out of nowhere knocking Dorek to his rear end in the dirt. He began to pull himself up when the Nazi grabbed him again. "You make one mistake and I will personally hunt you down and kill you. Do you understand?"

Dorek nodded his head still reeling from the blow. He would do as this Nazi asked.

The Nazi shoved him back to the fence. "Now get out of my sight!"

Dorek scrambled through the fence rushing to escape but stopped at the Nazi's voice. "Well cover up your hole, idiot! You can't do as I say if you leave a hole the size of your idiot head under the fence."

Dorek looked up, stunned. The Nazi sounded almost amused. He sure didn't find anything at all amusing about this situation. Well, except for the fact that he was somehow miraculously alive. He would be alive for at least one more day, depending on how well he could do the task assigned to him. He couldn't tell Henryck or Beatrice, or anyone else for that matter what he was to do. If they knew, they wouldn't allow it, and he would die.

"You've been wanting to talk to me about that mangy..." Klaus paused, thinking. He started again, "I've put some thought into it, and we need to talk about Eva."

Josef stopped chopping up the vegetables at the table. "Yeah. I had been thinking that too." Klaus waved a hand at him, impatiently. "I know. I know." He walked over to the table and poured two drinks handing one to Josef and downing the other. He exhaled slowly and met Josef's eyes.

"She's got to go. You know she does."
Josef nodded, he too knew this. For many months they had carried on this charade. He knew at some point it would have to end.

"Josef. She has to go!"

"I know."

"What do you propose we do with her?"

"What can we do? You brought her here. You think of something...but it has to be tomorrow."

"Why the hell tomorrow, Klaus? You couldn't have brought this up sooner and gave me a chance to figure out something?"

Josef watched Klaus's eyes narrow dangerously in his anger. He could sense a storm brewing; he could feel it in the air. "Wait..wait..wait. You go out and save some damn mangy ass kid, don't tell me anything about it and then you want to just settle down and raise a baby in a cesspool and never once question what *I* want?"

"Well, what *do* you want Klaus?"

"Oh! Now you get around to asking me when you turned my whole world upside down and risked my life to save some dumb kid!" Klaus strode to the window and paced back to Josef. "You know what I want? I want-"

"Well I just want you and Josef." Eva's small voice cut in. They hadn't seen her creep from her hiding place and take her place between them.

"That's because you're just a teensy stray kitty cat and you'd twist yourself through the legs of anyone that fed you and then you get them all tripped up with your great big eyes!" Klaus looked down at her and winked when he was sure Josef was not watching him. He'd be damned if he would let Josef see him go soft!

"So. You and Eva need to go. I'm going to get you to the other side of the fence. Eva, you will be as quiet as quiet can be. We're going to tuck you in a big bag with a bunch of clothes, and for god's sake, don't move in it."

Josef looked up at his friend. "So we're just going to walk right out the gate with an escaped prisoner?"

"No! Josef, you're an idiot! Where in the hell is your imagination? We're going to walk out of the gate with your duffel bag because your damned Aunt Helga fell and broke a hip and you need to run to her rescue or some other dumb shit."

Josef looked at Klaus, truly looked hard at him in the first time in months. While his friend was just as loud and obnoxious as always, he seemed to have aged a decade. Stress lines crossed his forehead, a map of all the places they had been together.

"Klaus, what do you plan to do?"

Klaus waved him off impatiently like he always did, when Josef or anyone for that matter bothered him.

"I'm coming back here and cleaning up the mess you made." Klaus strode from the room without looking back. His boots sounded on the porch stairs before they sounded again. He popped his head in the door. "Tomorrow at first light. I'm heading out on night patrol. Be ready."

Once more Klaus's boots walked away leaving Josef and Eva alone in the barracks. "Josef? Can I ask you a question?"

"Sure Kitten."
"Klaus isn't going to come with us?"

"No, but I'm sure he will eventually be with us."

"Will momma die?"

Josef was silent, he had thought very much the same thing. He had to figure out a way to get Hanna out and he had mere hours to orchestrate an escape.

"Stay here. Your mom will be ok. So will you. I promise."

Eva nodded silently and watched as Josef walked out the door, distractedly forgetting to lock it for the first time since Eva had come. Eva wandered back to the barracks bedroom and gathered up the small tablet Klaus had found for her to draw on.

Eva grabbed some paper and drew, quietly humming along laying on her stomach with her legs bent at the knee and wiggling her small toes in the air along with her humming.

She barely moved when she heard a loud alarm ringing in the distance. She smiled to herself as she colored on her paper. Usually when the alarm sounded, it meant someone got away. The other side of the fence meant good. This side of the fence meant bad, although Eva only thought about it in its simplest terms. She was well fed and exceptionally cared for, unlike millions of others.

Living through this horror and coming out the other side, she would realize as she grew up it wasn't a matter of who was better than anyone else. It was nothing like that. Many a time, rather than smarts or skills…which abounded in the camps, survival simply came via a whim. A sheer bit of luck. Eva just so happened to have that luck. She was one of the few that survived, and one of the very rare that survived better than most.

Lost in her thoughts, she didn't hear the footsteps by the bed until she heard the floor board creak. She looked up with a smile on her face and started to cover up her drawing she made of herself, Klaus and Josef.

Her smile immediately fell and she sat up, pushing herself as far back against the wall as she could away from the horrible sneering face that was glaring down at her.

"I always thought there was something Josef and Klaus *the great* were hiding. I just never knew it was a damned rat." The man moved closer to the bed, leaning over it to get even closer to Eva.

Eva's eyes widened as the man hovered over her. She knew him well. He was the one that always laughed and watched when Rissling used to beat her. She looked to the door to make sure Rissling wasn't coming in as well, even though she knew he was dead, though she didn't know how he had died.

"You're awfully well fed for a dead skeleton. It's going to be fun to drag you through the camp. I think, after I show you to the other guards, it will be fun to drag you over to your mom…and let her bury you twice."

Chapter 32

Eva looked toward the wall and back toward the door her quick mind trying to think of any possible escape route. She didn't realize it, but she knew not to even try to talk. Instinctively, she knew anything she did would just make this monster attack. Her mind reeled as she tried to think of anything she could do to escape.

She had been extraordinarily lucky up to this point. At least until this monster entered her sanctuary. She pushed farther into the corner pulling her legs up close to her body and laying her head on them, arms curling tightly around her knees. She squeezed her eyes closed, tears already flowing.

Her small shoulder felt like it would be ripped from her body as the man grabbed it and pulled her closer to him. "I'm going to enjoy the hell out of this" he sneered as he slapped her across the face. Before she could even scream from the pain and terror a gruff voice spoke.

"You touch that baby one more time and I blow your head off right now!"

Heinrich stood in the doorway to Josef and Klaus's bedroom his pistol aimed directly at Rissling's former 'right hand man'. His pistol never wavered as the man set Eva down on the bed. She slowly brought up her hand to feel the side of her mouth where the brute had struck her.

The man turned and faced Heinrich, the same sneer on his face. "I suppose you were in on this stinking rat cave too, huh?"

"As a matter of fact I wasn't. I simply owe them a favor. If that favor is in the shape of a child, so be it."

The men faced off. Neither speaking, the small child sat trembling. She would die this day.

"This is it! This has to be the spot!" Bertrain looked around excitedly. It truly didn't seem to faze him that he was in a war zone, with potential enemies around every curve in the road. His blue eyes twinkled toward the General and then he shaded his eyes with his hands, pointing to the top of a hill with the other hand. "There. That's where they'll come from. I'm sure of it."

Grayson shook his head. "We shouldn't even be here. If anything that's where the damn entire Nazi Army is going to come streaming over the hill...and then we all die!" He kicked a dirt clod and sighed. This was a fool's errand.

The General knew his men were on edge. To be honest with himself, he had felt the same way about 45 miles into their drive into war-torn Poland behind enemy lines.

Another soldier, Will, stepped up to the assembled men. "I think we're doing the right thing men. If that kid does come to be rescued, the least we can do is be there to catch her."

Bertrain nodded and looked around. "We made it here anyway. Any minute now I expect them to come. We'll be ok."

Grayson rolled his eyes. "You think everything is ok! It's damned irritating. For that matter you are damned irritating!" At Bertrain's deep shrug, Grayson took a deep breath in preparation to yell his thoughts of this wild goose chase at this damn irritating kid, when a voice called out...unseen in the dense brush.

"I am to speak with Bertrain and a General. No others."

The soldiers quickly aimed their rifles at the brush near the road. The bushes moved slightly again, "Please don't shoot. Just send Bertrain over. I have a package for only them."

Bertrain watched as Grayson set his finger lightly on the trigger, preparing to fire should he need too and glanced at Bertrain. "This is your shit show" he whispered harshly. Bertrain nodded, got approval from his General and slowly walked behind the trained rifles and began to walk toward the brush.

Slowly a young man walked through the brush, his hands up facing the American Soldiers. "I promise you I mean no harm, but I do have a package that I am to deliver to you and only you. Please take it from me. If I do not deliver it, I will be killed."

Bertrain and the General advanced slowly upon the young Polish man. He smiled nervously and looked down toward the ground behind him. Both Bertrain and the General stared in shock before turning their gaze back to the young stranger.

Of all the men assembled, only one leapt into action. Bertrain gently pushed the young Polish man out of the way and knelt carefully on the ground, a slight smile on his face. He looked back up at the young man. "We've got it from here, soldier."

Chapter 33

Josef and Klaus walked together back toward their barracks, both of them breaking into a dead run as they noticed the barracks door open.

Both men drew their pistols before heading into their open door. Klaus was first to step into the open bedroom door. He pushed past Heinrich on his way in. As soon as he laid eyes on Eva and the bright red blood on the side of her face he quickly turned back to Heinrich, his pistol aimed at Heinrich's forehead. "You dared to touch this child?"

Heinrich never flinched. Had he not been in such a life and death situation as he found himself in, he might have laughed. Klaus resembled an angry rooster with its neck feathers sticking straight out, ornery at the world. Klaus took a menacing step closer. Heinrich met his infuriated glare and nodded toward the corner of his room.

Slowly, Klaus took his eyes off Heinrich and looked toward the mentioned corner. Rissling's old friend and ally stood totally at ease in the corner; the grin slowly beginning at the corner of his mouth to widen.

"You aren't getting out of this alive, Strochmoer."

"That's where you are wrong. I owe them a favor. If the girl here is the price, so be it. You aren't touching them." While Heinrich spoke softly, his voice remained deadly serious.

Klaus walked past Heinrich and up to Rissling's old crony. He stood looking at the man for a moment. "You know. I never liked you." He pulled his fist back and connected hard with the man's jaw. His head flew back, striking the wall behind him before he slowly slid down the wall. He came to a stop on the floor and slumped over sideways, his head bent at an odd angle. "Shit. Did I kill the bastard?"

Josef walked farther into the room and looked down at the fallen officer. "No. He's still breathing." Klaus kicked at the man's leg.

"Well. What do we do?" Josef looked at Klaus and Heinrich.
"We get the hell out of here."

"I'll stay here for a few minutes, cover you, but that's all. I owe you. It's as simple as that."

Eva walked over to Heinrich and looked up at him. "Thank you." Then she turned to Klaus and Josef, put her hand up on her slim, but steadily growing hip. "It's about time you got here!"

Heinrich looked quickly to the two men, who seemed almost dumbfounded as well. Heinrich's whisker twitched suspiciously as Klaus stomped angrily off to the kitchen his back ramrod straight. It twitched again when Klaus returned with a washcloth and tossed it at Eva. "Wash your face off. You'll get blood all over."

Eva rolled her eyes and wiped her face, then looked back up at Heinrich again. She smiled up at him, blood staining her cheek near the corner of her lip. Heinrich looked at the child, staring up at him so trusting...and so different from the very few children that were alive in the camp. He bent down to her, took the rag and quickly wiped the last bit of blood off the side of her lip. He spoke softly to her, "Those two are always taking their time. You should try working with them. They're slow then too."

Eva looked over to Josef and Klaus and laughed. "I know."

Josef cleared his throat and motioned Eva back to her hiding spot. He gestured again and both the other men followed him to the kitchen. They stood in front of the door. No one said anything for a moment, until Heinrich spoke. "You gotta go boys. I'm covering for you, for now, and I'll try to hold them off as much as I can. When this guy wakes up, I'm going to be somewhere else, but you got time now."

The men simply nodded. It was time. Time to go, time to live or to die…but it was time to do something. They never looked back as they carried the rucksack of clothes and a hidden Eva out through the gate.

As they entered the outside perimeter, they relaxed only slightly. Klaus pointed, "We're meeting someone there. Where the river flows at the Y in the river bend. It's about three miles. We can't take a vehicle."

They looked back only once, when the rifles sounded and Klaus felt a tearing in his side. He met Josef's eyes only momentarily as both men broke into a run. Klaus faltered as he ran, Josef pulling him as much as he could.

They heard the shouts and the vehicles behind them, as they ducked into the trees. At least anyone on their trail would have to run through the woods too. Josef knew Klaus was hit, but he didn't know how bad it was.

They stopped only for a minute to take Eva out. She would have to run from here on out along with them. Josef couldn't carry her and Klaus. He hoped he wasn't making a decision that would cost the child her life after all this time. He had to help his brother.

The men struggled through another mile, getting closer to Klaus's destination, but the men behind them were sounding closer. Eva ran, ran as though she had never been half starved only a few scant months ago. She ran with the strength of a well taken care of child. A child it seemed, who had never been rescued from the arms of pure evil and delivered to a foul mouthed couple of unlikely angels to save.

Another slow and tortuous hill and valley fell beneath their feet as they stumbled, fell and ran toward what Klaus hoped would be their safety. There was only one last hill to go when Klaus fell, the wound in his side leaving a solid blood trail for the soldiers to follow.

Klaus stumbled and fell, the hand he had held over his wound stretched out in front of him. Moving leaves and streaking the forest floor with blood. He could go no farther. He left another large streak of blood, this time on his face as he wiped the sweat from his eyes. "Josef, you got to go. I'm sorry brother."

Chapter 34

"Kraus!! Kraus!" Eva screamed and ran back to the fallen soldier

"Kraus get up. Hurry Kraus, you have to come too"

Klaus looked up and saw his friend; his loyal brother run towards him and the child.

"Dammit Josef, get the fuck out of here!"

"I'm not leaving you" the tears rolled off Josef's nose as he screamed down at his friend. The tears left a clean path, the only clean path that was anywhere to be found.

"Dammit Josef, you can't save us all- you never could, don't you know that now? You're just too damned stupid to see it! They're coming. I'm not going to live anyway; you know that too…" Klaus took a deep breath and looked once more into the face of his friend. "get that little girl out of here, you stupid horses ass! GO!"

Josef grabbed Eva's arm and turned to run. Eva pulled out of his grasp and ran back to Klaus.

Despite the sounds of shots in the distance, and the occasional shout of one of the men following them, the forest was silent as the small Jewish girl knelt over the body of her friend, her protector; the Waffen SS guard.

"Eva! Get the hell out of here!" Klaus swatted her away as though a pesky fly and she fell to the ground. She scrambled up, crawled quickly back and cradled Klaus's head in her lap.

"I love you Klaus. I knew you liked me all along, even when you pretended you didn't" his sweet brown eyed Eva pressed her lips to Klaus's fore head. He gently smiled, hearing his name correctly for one of the first times, knowing it would be last.

"I know you did." The wounded SS grabbed the small girl and pulled her to his chest for a tight hug. The first and only time Klaus would ever hug his young charge. "You take care of Josef for me ok? He is a real dummy sometimes, and always messing shit up, you gotta keep a good eye on him, ok Eva? Will you do that for cranky old Klaus?"

He held the girl tight for another second and then lifted her from his chest. With effort he sat up despite the pain. He looked into her eyes and pressed his bloody lips to her forehead. He pulled away and looked into her eyes again. With one dirty finger, he wiped away a tear off the end of Eva's nose. "You take care of Josef for me." The girl nodded and placed her small hands on the SS soldiers face.

Eva nodded again and turned to Josef. Josef bent to grab her and scoop her up. Klaus waved a hand to stop Josef.

"Pull me to this tree and lean me against it. I can't fucking shoot laying down you idiot."

Josef knelt and hugged his friend, his brother and then lifted him to push him back against the tree. He kept his hands on Klaus's shoulders "I'm sorry, Klaus. Sorry for everything."

"Shut up you stupid fool. You were right all along. I'm sorry I didn't see it like it you did. But if I had, you'd never be in this cesspool saving that Eva girl. Which you're not going to do if you keep standing there hugging me like some faggot. Now get her the hell out of here." Klaus coughed, more blood and foam staining his lips, to drip down his chin.

The men shook hands one last time and broke apart as the whistle of a bullet whined overhead.

"Now get out of here. Get that stupid kid out of here."

Josef grabbed Eva on the run and she tried to squirm out of his hands. He managed to keep a hold of both her and his rifle but now she was twisted behind him.

"Eva! I love you too" Josef heard Klaus shout.

Klaus raised his hand farewell and Eva began screaming, "Klaus! Klaus" Her shrill screams broke his heart.

A minute later he heard Klaus's rifle discharge in a steady stream and then a volley of shots from the soldiers just breaching the clearing. Eva stopped screaming and went limp in his arms. The shouts got farther away as Josef ran, the soldiers looking through the brush next to his fallen brother for them. His old friend Klaus had bought them some time.

Josef hoped the car would be hidden right where it was supposed to and that Hanna had been able to make her way to it…or even believed him when she was ordered to meet him there.

As he topped the last hill to the road his heart sank, several vehicles were surrounding a small company of enemy soldiers. The accompanying soldiers all had their rifles pointed at him.

"Bring the girl here" a voice boomed in perfect English.

Behind Josef, shots rang out again. "I'm coming, don't shoot! I've got the girl."

Josef ran towards the vehicles. He had no choice. To go backwards was to be killed by 'his own men' for treason. To go forwards was uncertain. The only certainty was that any other direction, except maybe forward, was signing his death warrant.

Josef continued his run to the men at the bottom of the hill. As he got closer he could see United States insignia. A young marine grabbed Eva from him and swung his fist at Josef. "Filth! Murderer" The man struck Josef again and he fell, embarrassed; as he was both weak and exhausted from his emotional wringing out and the energy used on this run carrying Eva and pulling his wounded friend for so long.

A General strode up, taking his time as the young marine kicked Josef again. "Enough Lt! The man will stand on trial for his crimes! Men, get this maggot up."

"They're coming! Right behind me." Josef managed to sputter out

Eva jerked away from the marines grasp and ran to Josef. He bent to scoop her up and the surprised marine came at Josef with his fists up. The general halted the soldier with a hand raised.

"This could be a trap. Stand ready men!" he ordered. In a single movement all of the soldiers were behind the vehicles with rifles aimed at Josef and Eva.

Eva tucked her head under Josef's chin; he wrapped his arm around her, with a stained hand behind her head. "I'm Josef Roehm. There are Waffen coming. I stole this child from the camp. Her mother is still imprisoned there."

The U.S. General looked at Josef with disdain. "You think I was born yesterday you Nazi pig! The mother is here. You killed her daughter months ago! Not anyone else, YOU, Shutzstaffel , Josef Roehm. We have her mother here with us." The United States General turned to his men, "I am not giving an order nor a command, but if one of you wants to shoot this Nazi Waffen pig be my guest. There will be no court martial. I don't give a shit."

The young marine who had already struck Josef came forward. The bayonet of his rifle only inches from Josef's face. Eva squeezed tighter onto Josef, holding on with her arms and legs as another soldier tried to pry the girl off of Josef, her hands clenching his jacket tightly.

Eva screamed. A piercing, terrified scream. The hardened, battle worn men grimacing at the sound, and looking amongst each other; there was no reason for this lucky, sweet girl to hold onto one of the third Reich's own! Was there? What was going on?

Suddenly Hanna's voice came loud and clear, "Eva! EVA!" The men broke ranks and let the young emaciated woman through. She looked in disbelief into the eyes of the man she had hated. He dropped his eyes first and kneeled on the ground, several of the rifles of the U.S. Marines following his movements.

He carefully peeled the girl's legs from around his waist and kneeled until her small feet, encased in new shoes touched the ground. Hanna took a couple tentative steps forward. She was certain she had heard her daughter's voice, except this girl had shining beautiful hair-albeit shorter than she had ever had it…and Eva was dead. When Hanna had last held her thin Eva before the firing squad, her pretty girl had been just an emaciated waif, with eyes that seemed far older than their years. She had been ripped from her arms, by this very same monster, and told she was to be killed for her mother's transgressions. But there had been no fat on her baby girl's bones; her baby's hair was thin and brittle then. This healthy girl with the shining hair and round cheeks could not possibly be her Eva. Could she? She blinked tears back as she gazed upon the perfect young girl.

Hanna gazed upon this child, so much like her own Eva as curiosity, hope and disbelief crossed her face. She glanced up at the U.S. General who was carefully watching her reactions.

Josef carefully peeled Eva's arms from around his neck and brought both his large hands to each side of her head. The young Marine took a step closer, the tip of his bayonet aiming down just inches from Josef's left eye. He was ready to take down this Nazi pig if he kept threatening the girl. Josef dismissed him at a glance and then turned his attention back to his Eva.

An older marine, stepped to the young man and put a hand on his shoulder. "Stand down, Johnston son, I think you are seeing a miracle." Slowly, almost jerkily, the young soldier withdrew his rifle and set the butt of it next to him. His knuckles showed white, as the grip on his stock remained just as tight as it was before. The young man may have only been 19, but he had lived a lifetime of horrors in only the last year on German and Poland soil.

Josef pulled Eva a few inches closer. His left hand coming off the side of her head to comb back a stray tendril of hair off the girl's forehead. He grabbed her small hand in his and brought it to his lips. Slowly, he turned the young girl to face the crowd.

Hanna brought her fist to her mouth, not believing her eyes. She searched Josef's eyes and collapsed to her knees. Her baby was alive! Her baby was healthy! She slowly held up both of her arms weakly, not knowing if this was a dream. Scared to believe it, but knowing that if it was just a dream, it would pull the life right out of her.

Eva smiled and gave Josef's hand a tight squeeze then ran to her mother's arms. While Eva's arms quickly enveloped her mother's neck, Hanna's own arms were slow to surround her daughter. She was still so afraid that if she wrapped her arms close to this little entity that she would somehow disappear. She brought her tear filled eyes back up to those of the US General. He swept his hat off his bald head and smiled at her. A grandfatherly smile, and nodded with a smile.

Hanna turned back to Josef and stared into the face that she had hated for so many nights. How had this man…no… why had this man saved her daughter? She looked back into her daughter's sweet face. Eva smiled up and her and kissed her cheek. Hanna finally embraced her daughter, sobbing.

Some of the hardened soldiers looked away or walked to the other side of the vehicles, complaining about all the dust in their eyes. Hanna laughed through her tears, "Eva?"

Eva looked into her mom's eyes and laughed. A light, sweet bell in the dark of night... "Hi Momma. I'm six now! Josef said I couldn't even sneak around to see you or else someone would see me and we would all get in big trouble. Klaus..." Eva sniffed as her voice cracked, "Klaus tried to make me a cake, but he burnded it. Then he got mad and made me a sandwich and yelled at me, because he doesn't...." Eva sniffed again, "He never did like sandwiches. Or cooking. I think he only cooked so he didn't die. That's what Josef said."

Hanna looked again at Josef. "Klaus?" she mouthed the name. Klaus was one of the orneriest guards there. She had never seen him beat anyone, but he yelled non-stop and ordered everyone around. How and why would that jackal make her daughter a cake?

Eva turned in Hanna's arms and put a small hand over her eyes to shield them from the sun as she looked up at the old U.S. General. "Josef is my friend. He saved me. Momma too, but he said Momma couldn't know, else she might let the cat out of the bag. I never saw a cat thought."

That battle worn old soldier took his hat off and knelt to the small girl. He touched the healthy, happy girl's forehead with his grizzled work worn and stained index finger. "I bet you've got a lot of stories to tell up there in that pretty little noggin of yours." He stood back up and barked an order at his troops. "Get these three up there on the truck and get your rifles aimed over that hill. You see any more Nazi's you kill them all."

Eva pulled on the sleeve of the Generals uniform, he looked down at her, still awed at her powerful story of survival, "But not Klaus. Don't shoot Klaus. Ok? He's my friend."

The General looked over at Josef, questioning him with a raised eyebrow. Josef shook his head slowly. Klaus wouldn't be coming over the hill. The General saw the look on Josef's face and nodded. A battle ready soldier himself, he knew the look. The Nazi's comrade was gone. The Marines stood silently by, they too knew the haunted look that only a fallen brother could bring to his friends face. A few of them even took off their hats.

The young soldier who had first assaulted Josef, walked next to Josef and looked at the General. The General stood a moment, deciding and then nodded his head. "Men, train your rifles on that hill. I'm sure the Nazi's went back to their camp in hell, but shoot any you see. Grayson and Johnston take young Josef here to see to his pal."

The men nodded and set to follow orders. The General cleared his throat again, "Men, he gives you any trouble, don't let yourself get killed over him. You hear that, Nazi?"

Josef nodded and looked to the hill. He knew Klaus was gone, but at least he could give his friend a proper burial. Together the three men started toward the hill. Eva snuggled into her mother, Hanna wrapped her arms around her tightly until Eva squirmed and pushed against Hanna in order to be free from her tight embrace.

Chapter 35

"Momma, Josef tried to tell you I was ok, but you never listened to him. Where's Marta?"

Hanna sighed. With believing that her beautiful Eva had been lost to her, she had never even thought about ever having to tell Eva that Marta was gone. She looked at her daughter and was struck with a sudden inspiration. "What did Josef and Klaus tell you?"

"Oh Klaus and Josef were all crabby one night, so Klaus told me that Marta and her soldier friend ran away to get married and live happily ever after. Josef kept stomping around that day, then they made me hide under the bed when a soldier guy came. I almost sneezed, because the floor was really dusty. But then I went to sleep and they forgot about me until Klaus sat down. He almost squished me!"

Hanna hugged her daughter close. Those two hardened and cruel guards had protected her daughter not only physically… but they had protected her poor, sweet heart as well. Hanna smiled and put her hand on her daughters face. She looked up at the General and then back to her girl, before reaching out a finger to trace the curve of her face.

"Yes, my own brave flower. Marta and her soldier did live happily ever after."

"Can we visit them? Josef kept saying he didn't know how to find them, but then Klaus jumped in again," Eva sighed dramatically and kicked the small toe of her shoe into the dirt between their feet, "He said I wasn't 'sposed to grill you about Marta."

Hanna didn't know how to answer, so she said nothing. Perhaps later she would speak of Marta when she was not still recovering from the biggest shock of her entire life.

A younger soldier called to the General from the side of the hill and the General walked over. Hanna kept her eye on them to see if she could discern what the men were concerned about. Briskly, the General returned to Hanna's side. She stood and he placed his hand gently, but firmly on her elbow, steering her in the direction of the trucks. "Miss, let's get you two into one of the trucks." Hanna began to walk toward the truck when she caught a movement on the hill. Josef's Waffen blue uniform stood out from the US Army green of the two soldiers between them.

Hanna felt her daughter try to wrench from her grasp. She knew the Waffen SS had saved her daughter's life, but that still did not make her want to let her daughter run to this "monster" instead of hold on to her. She wondered for a moment if she would ever get over the feeling of loss, and in a way betrayal. Her daughter should run to her, not the man who had ran the concentration camp. She clasped her daughters hand tight, so tight her daughter tried to wrench away. Hanna couldn't let her daughter run back to the man she only knew as a monster, so she held tighter.

Eva struggled to wrench her grasp from Hanna's hand. When she couldn't do it by her own strength and they were behind one of the waiting trucks, Eva screamed. "Josef! Klaus! Help!!" and began in earnest to try to free herself from the tight grasp her mother had on her hand.

Hanna felt a loss akin to what she had felt when her daughter was first taken from her. This time though it was worse, because her daughter was reaching for a "monster" and pulling away from her own mother. Hanna's arms and hands went weak. Not only from the exhaustion had she endured from her time with in the camp, but from the heart in her heart. She felt the warmth from her daughter's hand as she finished pulling away and began running toward Josef...Josef the monster.

"Josef! Klaus!" The small girl ran toward the man she loved. The man who was "papa" in her heart.

Josef ran towards the advancing child, as he half carried and half drug the body of his fallen friend. Eva did not need to see any more horror than she already had. He gently sent his fallen brother down and resumed his run to the child.

Eva stood in the middle of the field. Josef, Grayson and Johnston silhouetted on top of the hill with dusk coming down. The US soldiers standing behind her, her mother with them. The small valley was quiet...too quiet and the girl stood in the middle not sure which way to go. A small sound from a small stand of trees went un-noticed by all gathered.

The tip of a black muzzle of a rifle slowly peeked out of the bushes around a large tree. It zeroed in on the girl and held steady as the child slowly turned and looked right at the rustling leaves. The girl went stiff and still as she noticed the barrel of the rifle trained on her. Josef watched Eva closely and followed her gaze. A glint of reflected sunlight and a slight movement had Josef tapping Grayson's arm. He nodded and gestured toward the bushes.

Josef waved at Eva to get her attention. He slowly brought his finger to his lip and pointed to her, then at the ground. Eva looked down to her feet and then back up at the soldier. He held up one finger for the girl to wait. When she went to nod he shook his head no. The minute she made a move the gunman in the woods would fire.

Hanna watched all the unspoken communication between the two and anger overcame her. She became to march toward her child, who was so enamored with the asshole who had ripped the heart from her chest so many months ago. She watched as he began flailing his arms around trying to motion her to stop. Inside her slight body the rage she had bottled up for so long was coming to the surface. She was taking her kid away from this terrible man.

The soldiers at the bottom of the hill took notice when Grayson knelt on top of the hill with his rifle aimed at the small patch of brush off to their left. Then they noticed Eva in the clearing standing still watching as Josef tried to communicate with her to get ready to drop to the ground on his command.

Grayson quietly moved to another angle, Johnston followed. Whoever was in the brush at the bottom of the hill did not know they were there. He couldn't see them…but they couldn't see him either.

Since the shooter had not shot yet, the men on the hill could only assume that the shooter was using the child as bait. The men on the hill were obscured by the trees and foliage, the shooter was waiting for either Hanna or one of the US soldiers to come to the child. Josef paused for a split second, he angrily watched as Hanna stalked closer to her child.

He had tried to tell that stubborn woman a million times over that her child was alive. He had risked his life to keep that baby girl alive, Klaus had given his life for this little girl and in one stubborn, backwards woman all their sacrifice and effort would be null. That stupid woman was going to get his adorable girl killed.

Despite his exhaustion, Josef Took off on a sprint toward Eva. He could only hope like hell that the soldiers at the bottom of the hill could figure out he wasn't out to murder anyone and wouldn't shoot him on his race down the hill, or that Grayson and Johnston could get a shot at the man in the bushes.

As he began his run, that damn infuriating woman began running toward Eva. If she reached Eva first they were both dead. He ran harder. Still motioning for Eva to hold still. He knew if Eva bolted the shooter would instantly shoot, her flight triggering the shooters instincts. The shooter could still not see him, but would see him any second.

Josef used every last ounce of his waning strength to run to the girl. 20 meters, 15 yards, 12 yards, the shooter could see him now. Hanna was almost Eva. Josef made it to about 8 feet away from Eva just as Hanna reached her daughter. He flung himself through the air and collided with Eva and Hanna just as a series of simultaneous shots rang out.

He felt the burning in his shoulder and the tug on the opposite side. He hoped like hell the bullet had not gone through his arm and right into the girl he had struggled so long, so fiercely to protect. They fell to the ground together. He rolled and cupped Eva's head beneath his large hand and rolled so she would land on top of him, instead of the other way around.

As they hit the ground, Hanna's breath was knocked out of her. She lay still just for a second until Josef rolled over on top of her and pinned her to the ground. She struggled to free herself until Josef reached up and pulled her more beneath him until she could barely move. Why in the hell weren't the US soldiers killing him? Why weren't they stopping him?

Footsteps sounded over the valley and she felt his weight being lifted off of her. To her surprise though, the men seemed to focus on Josef and Eva and didn't pause to do anything more than glance over her. What was going on? Why were they so concerned with the man who just assaulted her...and her daughter?

The murmurs of the soldier's voices reached her and she noticed the flurry of activity. She heard Josef's voice above the others, "I don't fucking care. Take her! Take her!"

Hanna sat frozen. What had happened? She stiffened as she saw a soldier carry a limp Eva at a run towards the waiting truck. The huddle of soldiers parted as they helped Josef stand. Blood stained his shoulder and ran down his uniform, his hand pressed over his wound; blood dripped between his fingers. She looked from Josef again to where the soldier had run with her daughter.

She looked back to Josef and shrunk away from his hate filled stare. She had seen her share of hatred in the camp. She spider crawled backwards from his advancing form and extremely angry face.

"Why didn't you STOP? Why did you keep ignoring me? You stupid girl! I did not save Eva just for some idiot like you to come by and get her KILLED! Klaus DIED for her!" Josef stepped closer to Hanna and Grayson, the young soldier blocked him. "She didn't know Josef. Leave her be."

Josef swore, and cursed her, the war, the Nazi Regime, Hitler all the way to the vehicles. She was too afraid to walk closer to Josef. The anger and hatred on his face was nearly palpable. She could feel how much he hated her. She walked even slower as they reached the vehicles. Her baby looked dead and had not made a sound. How cruel would the fates be to find her daughter alive and then have her killed for real just moments later? Hanna sank to her knees, and then placed her hands on the ground in front of her.

She couldn't take another single step. Maybe she would be lucky and God would just take her from all this pain right here and now. The old General walked to her side. He pulled her up to her knees and helped her stand. He pulled her to the back of the old Army Jeep where her Eva lie softly, angelic, on a soldier's flak jacket.

Chapter 36

Her beautiful face was that of a porcelain doll. Perfect features, that upturned nose, red cheeks on which lie some of the longest and enviable eyelashes. Hanna sobbed and brought her fist to her mouth to stifle the rest of the sobs as she saw the blood red stains on her girl's chest. Oh God, had she been killed?

She could hear Josef still yelling from the other vehicle a few lengths down. "Let me go. Let me go to her!"

"Will you just hold still you damn fool and let us at least get that hole plugged?" The old General swore again and chuckled. "There, you stubborn Nazi ass."

The huddle of soldiers parted again and Josef strode out, still holding the bloodied bandage over his shoulder. The men had cut the sleeve off his Waffen uniform. The strong, corded muscles stood out on his arm. Almost as much as his clenched jaw showed tight upon his face as he walked past Hanna barely sparing her a glance.

He walked to the small girl on the back of the truck and pushed the US soldiers out of the way. While he didn't shove Hanna out of the way, she felt as though he did by his stiff and cold indifference to her. Not that she wanted him to notice her, but as much as she was uncomfortable as she was in the presence of the SS guard, she found herself even more uncomfortable with his cold indifference.

"There are no wounds on her, Roehm. None that we can find anyway." A young soldier spoke up

"May...maybe she hit her head when we fell." All the soldier's eyes turned as Hanna spoke. At all their attention, Hanna down cast her eyes.

" Nien. She did not hit her head on the way down" Josef said, not as roughly as he had spoken to her before. Hanna looked up and met his blue grey eyes. Josef turned back to her baby.

He put his ear over her chest, then stood back and smiled as he had heard her heart, fluttering away in her chest. Hanna watched him. She braved the SS and softly put her hands around his forearm. He looked first at her questioning gaze and then winked at her. Hanna dropped her hands, why was he going to wink at her? What fool was this man! Hanna looked up at him again. Angry he would try to flirt or whatever he was doing while her baby was prose and obviously lifeless on the back of the truck. Even the assembled soldiers seemed uneasy with this most unusual turn of events.

Josef carefully placed his large hand on the small of Hanna's back. Slowly he guided her to the back of the truck. Respectfully, the soldier in front removed his hat and let Hanna through. She stood at the small hands and fingers of her child, laying so still next to her body. Hanna picked up her daughter's hand as was shocked. She had been prepared to touch a rapidly cooling body, and was amazed at the warmth emitting from that small hand and fingers.

She looked again into Josef's face. He winked again at her and put a finger to his lips admonishing her to remain quiet. She didn't know what to think or what to do, as this tall and tough SS guard leaned over the face of her baby girl.

She moved closer as Josef turned her daughters head carefully so her ear lined up to his lips. Hanna pressed her body against Josef's to see what he was doing. Her worry and curiosity overcoming her dislike for this most unusual man. Josef smiled at her for the first time and then whispered into her daughter's ear, "Mein kleines katzchen" The SS spoke. Her daughter's dark eyes opened immediately and she broke into a wide smile. Then lacking any sense of fear or hesitation, the girl reached up and hugged the SS, surprising some of the assembled soldiers. He picked her up. "Mein kleines katzchen".

Hanna looked up in wonder at this enigma of a man. She wasn't the only one; the young Grayson stood on Josef's right, opposite of Hanna and gave the Nazi a questioning look. "Josef smiled again, his hand firm but soft on the back of the head of the youn girl in his arms. He held his Eva out in front of him, so they were face to face. "Mein kleines katzchen" and they touched noses. The happy girl who had seemed lifeless only moments before smiled and giggled. She looked around and saw her mother and reached her hands out. Josef turned and handed Eva to Hanna. She slowly reached her arms out to take her child, and Eva grabbed around her neck with her arms and held her tight, snuggling the top of her head under her mom's chin.

Josef turned back to Grayson, "Long story. Short of it is, Klaus taught her to play dead, in case she was ever discovered with us after we took her. Mein kleines katzchen is 'my little kitten'. It was a joke between Klaus and Eva. He..." Josef looked at Hanna and even seemed somewhat chagrined as he continued the story he had started, "He always referred to Eva as a stray cat, and it became their pet name, Kitten."

Hanna felt her eyes tear up. These two awful men had protected her child from every possible danger? The weakness Hanna had felt for so long finally caught up to her as she realized they were all safe and they weren't going to be in camp anymore. She just couldn't seem to stand anymore and wobbled on her feet. A young soldier stepped forward to grab Hanna and Eva, but before he could Josef shot the man a murderous glare and swept the now unconscious Hanna and laughing Eva up into his arms. The US General hid a laugh behind a closed hand, as though he coughed and Josef glared at him for good measure too. The General chuckled again and pointed Josef toward the ambulance. He bade them all get in.

The War was far from over, the remaining camps would be liberated too far in the future to save many, but the allies had arrived. The tide was turning. The US General hopped in his jeep and smiled at Johnston walking back to his. "Well, son you've seen it all today. Nice shooting of that sniper, soldier. You did great. Only a few of you noticed him. Reckon we owe that Nazi something for the warning. You very well could have saved a lot of lives back there. So could he."

The General and Lieutenant Bertrain followed the ambulance along with the other vehicles. The headed away from Lublin Poland and hopefully towards a new life for Eva, Hanna and Josef.

Chapter 37

The trucks rumbled into the US barracks. Josef wasn't sure what was going to happen to him. A few miles into their journey, Hanna had woken up and seen him there. She had watched him with her hazel eyes for a few minutes before giving him a soft light smile and falling back to sleep. Eva had switched from his lap to sitting next to her mother on the floor of the US ambulance and chattering non-stop.

"Josef, where are we going? When are we going to get there?" She was just a bounding ball of energy. As tired as he was, his patience with his young charge won the respect of a soldier about his age named Will. "I've got two boys and a new baby girl back home in Georgia. This little one makes me wonder what my girl will be like, when she gets a bit older."

After a time, Eva crawled into Josef's lap and snuggled in. He winced as he brought his arm around the shoulders of the sweet, small girl. Dark haired Will had offered to hold her for him, but Eva became uncharacteristically shy and hid her head and face under Josef's chin. He leaned back against the wall of the rough riding vehicle and sought to find some respite from the bone deep weariness he felt. He held the girl close and closed his eyes after her deep and even breathing told him she was asleep.

He didn't know how long it had been, but he was awoken by a light tapping on his shoulder. He opened his eyes to find Hanna's gaze on him from the cot and Will next to him. Will had taken some of their jackets and blankets and made a bed for Eva. Josef bent to lay her in the makeshift bed, but found his arm pained him and was stiff as hell. Will met Josef's glance with his own questioning one. Josef looked down at Eva for nearly a full minute before he met Will's gaze again and nodded. He would let this US soldier take his girl. Will smiled and carefully took the sleeping child from the SS. Josef watched Will as though he were a hawk and Will a mouse in a field.

This was new for him. Before it had just been him and Klaus. He knew that no matter what Klaus's feelings, especially in the beginning, that somehow Eva was still safe with him. This stranger, the enemy, a US soldier, he wasn't sure about.

Satisfied that Will had not woken or disturbed the sleeping child, Josef leaned back into his corner of the hard ambulance wall again. He glanced at Hanna's bed and met her gaze. She smiled that pretty, sweet smile again and he found himself blushing.

He hadn't blushed in years, not since he was just a dumb kid first enrolled in the army. Now this scrap of a woman had him blushing like a school boy. He wasn't entirely sure he didn't like it, but he sure didn't want to be doing it in front of this US Army Lt. Will. Josef glared at Hanna and she smiled at him. He glared again for good measure and then closed his eyes, willing his facial color to go back to normal. Fortunately, he didn't hear Will laugh or he would have been pretty surly about it. Either Will just didn't care, as he should, or he never noticed.

In reality, Will had watched and had felt a catch in his heart. He sure was no romantical-notioned feller given his own past, but it pulled his heartstrings to watch their brief interlude. There may or may not be something brewing there, but with a sweet and bubbly girl like Eva in the middle, he did wonder how this would all play out.

Hanna closed her eyes again and thought back to the SS guard blushing. She didn't know why, but the thought made her heart hurt. For the last six months of drudgery and pain she had hated the man dozing across from her now. He was the one who had ripped her child from her arms and told her in front of the entire assembled Waffen that her child would be killed. He had left, one gunshot and her life was never the same. He had come back in about five minutes with the body of her child, wearing the same stupid uniform dress with the stained hem. She saw her daughter's body gets unceremoniously dumped into the mass grave.

She had screamed and shrieked and the ever cruel Klaus had hit her to stop her pitiful wails. Somehow she had staggered to the barracks and fell onto her bed. Marta had been there, sporting yet another fresh bruise over her eye and had rocked her to sleep as though she were just a babe.

Over the months, she would find her will to live would leave her. The cruel world, was simply no place to be. She had seriously considered just slowly walking away from her barracks towards the fence and just walking right into it. Either the electrical current or the impending bullets into her back would stop her pain. She just couldn't though. Even with her entire reason for living dead in the ground and decomposing back to earth and mineral, she still couldn't end her own pain. Perhaps it was just a punishment she had taken upon herself. A terrible punishment she gave to herself for living and for letting her beautiful child down. A punishment to make her stay alive and suffer when all she wanted to do was lie down and give up on this hell she knew as her life.

Even now, as she gazed upon the face of her child, she didn't know how she managed to survive. How either had managed to survive. She yearned to ask Josef why he had done what he had done. Why would he save just her girl? Why didn't he use his clout and save the entire community? Selfishly, she was glad he didn't do the latter, but why did he choose just one child. What did Klaus even have to do with anything? Klaus was an ass and she couldn't be sure that she wasn't happy he was finally dead.

As though her thoughts of the dead Klaus conjured her daughter awake, Eva moaned in her sleep and began to thrash. "No. no. no. Klaus. Klaus!" the tired girl shrieked in her sleep. Hanna pulled her daughter close to her and comforted the only way she knew how, by shushing and singing a light lullaby. So happy to have her baby safely in her arms again as she held her, she never even considered that her daughter wouldn't be hushed by her. It never entered her mind that her daughter might not want her to hold her.

Hanna held her crying and thrashing daughter while tears coursed down her cheeks. She didn't realize how hard she had been holding her child until she felt a light touch on her shoulder. It was Will and he held her gaze for a second before holding out his hands to take her child from her. Hanna didn't want to let go, and she felt like a terrible failure yet again that she couldn't console her own child. She glanced at that Waffen Guard in the corner. He still slept on through the crying and the rough rattling of the ambulance over the old dirt roads.

Hanna finally let her hold on Eva let go and Will pulled the crying child from her. He sat the girl on his lap and rocked her for a few moments. Eva refused to be quieted down and her cries became louder. Hanna looked to Josef again and found him slowly moving as though coming awake. Hanna was angry that this man was the reason her daughter didn't want her. Watching him sitting across from her, how easy it would be to just open the door and let him fall out and let the fall and nature do the rest.

As though he read her thoughts those blue grey eyes opened and stared into hers for a second. She watched as they narrowed dangerously as he turned his eyes to Will holding Eva. Eva wailed again, "Klaus!" The sound softened into another heartbroken sob. Will smiled at Josef. "It's ok. I was just trying to keep her from crying so you could sleep." Josef looked back at Hanna and saw her defeated pose and felt for her. That feeling only lasted for a split second until Hanna looked up at him with hatred and anger. He glared back at her, didn't she know that if it wasn't for him both she and her daughter would have been dead…and not in a peaceful way either.

He dismissed her with a quick shake of his head. "Eva. Stop crying. Come here." He spoke gruffly, much the same as Klaus had spoken to the girl in their barracks.

The girl nodded, sniffed and wiped the snot off the end of her nose with the back of a balled fist. Will let go of her and she stood awkwardly in the moving vehicle and walked toward Josef. He reached his good arm up as she got close.

"Josef, I want Klaus. Why isn't he here yelling at everyone?" Eva sobbed again and crawled into his lap.

Josef pulled the crying girl into his lap. "I will miss Klaus too. He sure yelled a lot didn't he?' Eva nodded, still sobbing as she snuggled closer into Josef's chest. She sniffed several more times and looked up into Josef's eyes. The Waffen SS looked down into her deep brown eyes and smiled. "Klaus was our good friend wasn't he?" Eva said quietly, barely able to be heard above the noise of the truck.

Josef pulled the girl back into his embrace, the pain in his arm from the bullet, less than the pain in his chest from losing his brother. "He sure was, little kitten. He sure was."

The rough rolling of the truck down the road lulled them both to sleep. Eva softly snoring wrapped in Josef's arm. Hanna watched them, her heart in shreds. She should hate this man…but her daughter loved him. For some stupid reason, her daughter- no her baby, loved this horrible man, and his stupid dead friend.

"General, Sir. Permission to speak freely?" Bertrain sat next to the General in the rolling truck. The General glanced over quickly, nodded and settled his eyes back on the dirt trail they were using as a road.

"What really happened back there, Sir? Why did that Nazi save the baby?"

The General took a breath and thought over what words he would use. Out of all his men, Bertrain the odd kid from Kentucky, seemed to overthink everything. He was never satisfied until he figured out whatever he was working out in his mind. He found quickly that Bertrain needed all the information he could get. If not, Bertrain would focus on whatever was working him up, much to the chagrin of all his comrades.

"Son, back there we said it was a miracle. Maybe it was. But, Bert the bottom line is that, the man had a heart. I can't imagine anything more terrible than being in a position like he was. To kill mercilessly-he may or may not have; but to have a heart to save at least one life. That man risked his life, and even now might be killed for whatever crimes he committed in there. I'll speak up for him though, if I can. He saved two lives, and he also saved ours back there. No, son, I would never want to be in his spot. For a man to only be able to save a few while thousands are being murdered around you."

Chapter 38

It would be another five years until Eva saw Josef again after their last memorable day at the US army camp. She never forgot Josef or Klaus and his constant yelling. Many a time, Hanna had been exasperated by her daughter. Not only had she survived a concentration camp- where by all means she should have perished, but she came out strong and tough...and with a terribly foul mouth.

Often Hanna had been forced to reprimand Eva's mouth. Over the years though, the reminders had become less and less. Even so, every once in a while when Eva thought she was alone, Hanna would hear her yelling curses at whatever she was presently working on. Hanna was convinced some of the things that came out of her daughter's mouth would make a sailor blush...but not a Nazi. A Nazi monster had taught her daughter to curse. He wouldn't blush.

Hanna would never know why that foul mouthed guard had saved her daughter, she didn't care. She could never forgive him for simply being an arrogant SS guard and Klaus to her epitomized her and her fellow inmate's pain. He, Klaus and his cronies were the cause of it all.

Although one day, Hanna had found out all that Klaus had done. That day she had felt for him, and for Josef, but over the years in America she had found herself feeling the same stirrings of hatred over Josef and Klaus. Especially when she had to reprimand Eva for her constant yelling and swearing!

Hanna sat on the porch in her house in the warm Georgia sun and sipped a cup of cool lemonade as she remembered the last time she had seen Josef.

Once Hanna and Eva had arrived to the US camp miles and miles away from Majdanek, they had been whisked off the truck. Soldiers had immediately taken Hanna and Eva to the medical ward. The nurses would look pitying in Hanna's direction and had delighted in Eva's health and vibrant personality.

The hardest thing for Hanna was listening to her daughter cry for Josef and Klaus. While in the camp, Eva had barely made a sound. She knew, and she had been told to keep as silent as she could, lest she be seen.

Now these horrible men were objects of her daughter's affection and tears. She was glad her baby had lived, and even that Josef and Klaus had saved her, but she didn't want to watch her child cry over demons.

Eva would beg the nurses to take her to Josef. Sometimes they did, once they were out of Hanna's sight. Josef was always happy to hold Eva and they talked for a couple minutes every few days. Josef had taken on the role of "full traitor" to his countrymen and had managed to stay out of the Russian prison he was to be sent to, by providing information to the United States about the camps and the regime. He had limited knowledge however and was nearly horrified when he found out how widespread the concentration camps and genocide of the Jewish population had been.

Josef was also surprised to hear how the Germans were actually losing. On maps, Bertrain and Grayson had showed Josef how they had stormed through and obliterated German holdouts on the way. Josef could only shake his head, he had no idea. News from his German commanders had trickled into him in Majdanek and was showing how brilliantly his soldiers were fighting, how they had fought back against the allies and were winning!

A month and a half in the US camp and Hanna was feeling as good as she remembered feeling in a long time. The Dr.s and nurses had been careful to feed her only small, light portions until she was able to begin to digest more and her starved body was ready to begin eating again. It had been a long process, one initially helped by the anonymous German Guard who had left small tidbits of food occasionally while she was imprisoned. Sometimes that wonderful bit of food came at a time when the whole barracks had been punished. They surely would have starved if not for that. She would never know of the one who had given them the extra food now and then.

Hanna told Eva about it one night when they were sitting in the hospital bed. They had laughed together about Marta waking up and smelling food. "Marta moved around some and so I opened my eyes, then her pert nose started twitching like a hungry bunny rabbit!" Eva giggled, remembering her friend Marta and imagining her nose wiggling around.

"You know, dear heart, on the day of your birthday we got food too. It was two sandwiches. Two great big sandwiches, but when we started eating them they tasted like they had been burned, but they had never been cooked."

Eva laughed for only a moment and then burst into tears and ran out of the hospital ward, blindly heading away from her mother. Hanna leapt out of her bed and followed behind her daughter. Try as she might, she couldn't keep up with the healthy, well fed girl. She found she was out of breath after the first couple of tents they passed. It would still be months until she would regain her former vigor.

Eva had run, tears clouding her eyes until she ran into Will, the nice guy from the truck. He picked her up and held her close although she didn't wrap her arms around him. She just hung limply from his arms.
"I want Josef. Please take me to Josef"

"Well, I don't know Darling."
Eva pulled back from Will, trying to escape his grasp realizing that he was not going to take her to Josef. "No! No! Josef!" The fiesty girl screamed and squirmed to get out of his grip.

The sound of running feet and shouts from his fellow soldiers had Will spinning around. Grayson, the General and Josef were running toward him. Grayson and the General were well behind Josef who was closing in on Will fast. Will realized the danger he could be in, should Josef believe he was trying to abscond with the girl. Thinking quickly, he set Eva on the ground and said loudly, "There he is. Old Will got you to Josef anyway, didn't he?"

Josef didn't look the least bit as though he believed Will, but he did stop running and walked over to Eva. She ran to him, arms outstretched just as Hanna finally caught up with her.

"Eva! Get away from that man!" She yelled, bracing herself up against an electrical pole for support, the energy drained from her run, gasping for breath. She watched helplessly as Eva looked over at her once and then continued her run to Josef.

He knelt on the muddy ground and embraced the girl. He pulled her tightly to him, missing the feeling of her in his arms. She tucked her head beneath his chin and he brushed her hair down on her head. "What's wrong honey?"

She sobbed a couple more times before she cried out again. "I miss Klaus!"

"I know honey. Me too."

"He was my friend."
"Mine too. How come you're so upset?"

"Momma was telling me about when it was my birthday and she ate a sandwich."

Hanna was now near the pair. She was just reaching to grab her daughter when Eva had mentioned the sandwiches. What on Earth got into her girl to go running away crying, *looking* for a monster over a damn sandwich?

Hanna was tired of this whole thing. The infatuation with this demon man! She was tired of it! She could do something about it now! She wasn't starved and beaten into submission anymore. She was going to end this here and now!

"Eva! Get over here now!"

Eva looked over at her mom and nestled closer into Josef's arms. Her small fists were grabbing handfuls of his jacket and then releasing. Josef pulled her into a tight embrace. He understood to some extent the feeling Hanna must be having, but couldn't she see her daughter was hurting...and that her daughter had lost a friend too. Was she so blind in her rage, that she just didn't see how much or how badly her daughter was hurting?

Josef pulled his head away from Eva's and looked directly into Hanna's eyes. He glared at her for a moment before turning away and walking towards the old General. "We need to settle this now. This child deserves more." The General nodded and beckoned Hanna follow them as the men began to walk towards the General's tent.

Hanna followed quietly. Not that she necessarily felt like being quiet. Quite the opposite, but she would see what this cad had up his sleeve and then she would drop her own bomb on him. Her and Eva's papers had been filed and returned and she would be heading to America soon, away from this awful place and this terrible man. He would never again disgrace her with his presence.

Even though they were no longer in the camp and he was no longer 'in charge' of her...she couldn't escape the feeling that it was still hunter and prey between them. She felt as though she should cower when he would walk past. Try as she might to understand her young daughter she simply couldn't see what her daughter even wanted to do with this man! It infuriated her to no end, and she was glad their time together was almost over.

The General opened the door to his tent, next to the large Red Cross tent and bade them all step inside.

Josef had watched Hanna often enough to know that she was keeping something from him. The woman thought she was so crafty, yet he always knew when she was up to something, it was all but written on her face. The woman could never play poker, that's for sure. He sure wouldn't want her as his partner.

Her constant whining about Eva seeing him infuriated him too. What more could he damn well do to talk some sense into her? He already risked his life to save her child and she still acted as though he were Rissling reincarnated!

He was getting sick of her high handed-ness. Had he ever hurt her in there? Had he ever done anything but save her dumb ass? Yeah, he knew he had to act cruel, but the end result was that she and the child were alive! Damn stupid woman!

Hanna glared at Josef's back. The self-righteous, arrogant fool thought he could look down on her. She had an ace in the hole. She was getting out of here and he would never again see her daughter! Everything was packed already and she had been careful not to mention it or discuss the move to America with Eva, lest she talk and let Josef know they were leaving.

Bertrain entered the tent, just as they were sitting around the General's table. The General shook his head, damn but that kid had a radar for anything interesting. He was always just popping in. He walked over to Josef and pinched young Eva on the cheek. She stuck out her tongue at him and Bertrain stuck his tongue back out at her and added one more. He stuck his thumbs in his ears and waggled his fingers at her.

Before this whole meeting turned into a kindergarten insult class the General cleared his throat. "What's the problem, Miss?"

All eyes turned on Hanna and she sat, shocked. This isn't what she had planned. The General all but turned this whole thing around on her, when Josef was the one who wanted to bring this all up! Slowly she stood; forcing herself to remember that no longer was she a half starved and half dead prisoner of war… she was Hanna Loev! The strong, independent widow that defied the Nazi regime for years and LIVED to tell the tale! She cleared her throat, and from her new vantage point, standing tall she glared down her nose at the pompous fool!

"Someone has been bringing *my* child to see this…this man, and I'll not have it any longer!"

The men sat quietly, several of them had brought the entreating girl to Josef. It was hard to resist such a cute voice and face begging them to take her to the nice man that had saved her life.

The General sat back, not exactly sure where to begin. Certainly, it wasn't to tell this woman that the young Nazi that saved her daughter's life *should* be able to see the child and the child him. If he knew anything at all about women these last 56 years on earth, it was never to jump between a mother protecting her child. Perhaps a different tactic could still yield the same result.

"Eva, why were you crying and running away from your mother?"

Chapter 39

Eva scooted quickly out of Josef's lap and over to the General. Many times she had been in the company of the grandfatherly General and had no qualms about climbing into his lap. Once seated to her satisfaction, she turned to the assembled group of soldiers, her mother and *her* Josef.

"Momma was telling me a story about when she and Marta woke up to find sandwiches in their bunk. She laughed about it and it made me mad."

"I didn't laugh at it Eva!" Hanna sharply spoke to her daughter

"Yes you did momma!"

Hanna sighed. Her daughter was a stubborn thing, that was a fact, and there was no way, in front of these men, especially Josef, was she going to get into a shouting match with the child. She decided to switch up the discussion and began to open her mouth to speak when Josef spoke.

"Katzchen, what has you so upset about the sandwiches?"

Eva sniffed a few times before talking. Hanna rolled her eyes; the damn Nazi pig was just trying to make her look bad!

"Josef, 'member when Klaus baked the cake and it got all burned and then he threw it in the trash and stomped all over the place yelling?"

"I do. He sure was angry. I don't think the smell went out of the house for days did it?"

"No!" Eva giggled "It was so stinky and every time the oven got turned on then the house would smell burnt again then Klaus would yell even more!" Eva laughed again at the fond memory of the man she had loved as a surrogate uncle or older brother.

Hanna had listened, her mouth slightly open and snapped it closed. Later, she would remember her outburst with embarrassment, but at the moment she was furious! How dare her very own flesh and blood and this heinous outsider trade stories and talk about home! It wasn't a damn home at all! It was the commander of the death camps own personal stall in hell!

"HOW DARE YOU! How dare you sit there and trade stories with my daughter like you have any right to be in her life! How dare you!"

Josef abruptly stood, the chair first scooting back and then falling over. He placed both hands on the table and leaned towards Hanna, a bit of hair falling over his forehead, "You both are only alive because of Klaus and I! Now Klaus, my brother is dead because of YOU! The child he gave his life for wants to stop by now and then and say hello and you freak out! YOU are the reason my brother is gone!"

Hanna stepped back at the ferocity of his words, and remembered that she was no longer a shirking coward. She leaned across the small table towards him and slapped him across the face as hard as she could. "You are the reason millions are dead! You are the reason that your buddy Klaus is slaughtered and I'm glad he's dead, I hope he is rotting in hell!"

"No!! No!" Eva wailed, trying to cover her ears and shake her head at the same time. She squirmed to get away from the General, but he maintained a hold on her, knowing that she was prone to run and damn fast at it too.

Josef sat back down, speaking once more before Hanna even had a chance. He knew how sensitive his girl was, not even bothering to think that she was not in fact his little anything, much less his child.

He used, as he always did when Eva was overly upset, Klaus's old way of speaking to her. "Eva" He ordered gruffly. "That's enough now."

Of all the men assembled, only Bertrain didn't even bat an eye at Josef's brusque voice towards the girl. He had watched closely the interaction between the young former prisoner and Josef, the guard tasked with killing her once.

He stood and looked over the assembled soldiers, the Nazi war prisoner, the baby and the harried mother. He cleared his throat and drawled his deep

Kentucky drawl, "How many times did you get extra food delivered to you, Hanna?"

Hanna, looked from her glaring contest with Josef. She blinked a couple times as though to clear her mind. "Wh- what? I don't know. A few I guess."

The men sat quietly, wondering where this unusual line of questioning was going. "So you thought Eva was dead right? They told you she was dead...you saw her dead, right?"

"Well, yeah. She was dead, as far as I knew. The body was wearing Eva's clothes. I was told she was dead. Where is all this coming from? I don't want to relive it."

The General watched carefully. Never had Bertrain spoke so much. He knew the young Hanna was flustered, and rightfully so. He stroked his mustache thoughtfully, but let the young man continue. He chuckled inwardly. If only he had a gavel and a robe, young Bertrain would make a good lawyer...if he ever got to the point.

"How often was food delivered to you before you were told your child was gone?"

"Well, none really, except for when the whole barracks got extra."

"Did you ever wonder where that food came from or who was doing it?"

"Well, yes but...we were so hungry that it didn't matter."

"Why did Eva get upset about the sandwiches? And that was on her birthday?"

"This whole line of questioning is getting us nowhere. This is ridiculous!"

The General shook his head and searched his mind for a Judge-ly thing to say. Nothing came to mind, he hadn't been to very many trials and he wasn't a terribly imaginative fellow, a fact his grandkids mentioned to him several times. He scratched his temple, stopping after a split second, "Get to the point Counsel!"

Bertrain looked over at him and winked, "Yes your Honor!" The kid knew all along what he had been thinking. Bertrain chuckled and looked over at Eva. "When we found you, you said Klaus made you a cake, but then you had sandwiches right?"

Eva shook her head and bounced her small pigtails up and down. Josef looked across the table at Hanna. She sat stoically, yet her eyebrow was raised in thought.

Bertrain let the assembled crowd think on that small tidbit of information, before he went on looking directly at Josef. "Close your eyes. You too Eva." Eva instantly closed her eyes, it was like a game. Josef glared even harder at Bertrain. Bertrain moved to Josef and gestured to Lt Grayson sitting there. Once the chair was vacated, Bertrain sat next to Josef, "It's cool. We ain't gonna kill ya. If we was gonna do that, we already woulda done it. Ya know?" Bertrain drawled to the German soldier.

Josef let out a wry grin and nodded. He too was curious where this line of questioning was heading too. Josef closed his eyes and waited. This was not at all a choice activity for him. A soldier never closed his eyes while on duty, at least not to play a kid's game. Especially in the company of what were in fact enemy soldiers.

As though reading his thoughts a voice rang out. Klaus's voice rang out. "Don't sit with your eyes closed you fool!"

At his old friends voice, Josef's eyes sprang open, already filling with tears he had yet to shed for his old friend. He met Bertrain's eyes and smiled.

Bertrain stood again, I think I can clue you all in. He turned to Josef, "This was classified information, but I'm sure you are wondering how we came to be here. Let me start with Hanna."

"Hanna in your testimony you captured by the villagers and forced to march an entire day at top speed to meet with us. Yet, you never wondered why." Hanna slowly nodded, still perplexed.

"Eva, you were told that you and Josef were heading toward a new home right?" Eva nodded again, "Klaus said we were."

"General, can I get your file folder on Josef?" Intrigued, the General handed over the information quickly, just as curious as the rest of the soldiers.

"Hanna can you describe Klaus to the best of your ability?" Bertrain studied a piece of paper from the file before turning back to Hanna. He raised an eyebrow.

"Well, he is…was… tall, with sandy blond hair and blue eyes. You just looked at him and saw evil. Nazi incarnate!" Hanna hissed. Bertain looked back to the file in his hand. "Would you call him tall, blue eyed with laugh lines running around his cheeks and deep forehead lines?" Hanna nodded slowly.

"Would you also call his voice 'sort of gravely and gruff'" Bertrain quoted the paper in his hand. "Well, yes but-" Bertrain held up a hand to stop Hanna's talking.

"A villager described a man I just described to you. He said he was helping prisoners escape, when an officer matching this description told him to get you, and bring you to us…although he did not tell the villager who you were going to meet."

A small dawning of thought began to creep into Josef's mind. "He told me where we were going, but only said there would be a car waiting for us. He never mentioned an entire United States Army Platoon."

Bertrain walked over to the General. "Will you tell Josef and Hanna…" He paused, "And our Eva here what the German soldier said when he contacted you?"

The General cleared his throat and stood. "He said he was chasing down a German traitor who had kidnapped a young child and he was meeting the mother at our location to kidnap her as well." The General looked once more at Josef, "He said he was to kill the escaping traitor and that he would die trying."

Bertrain turned to Grayson, "You were ready to kill Josef when you first saw him. Why was that? You knew he was kidnapping a child from an internment camp." Grayson looked shocked; he was simply enjoying the trial like experience and hadn't counted on being drawn into it. "Well, it was the way the German talked. He talked like he was a friend to this German traitor and I thought it was a trap to lure us in."

Bertrain nodded, "It was a trap." Bertrain sat down, all of the assembled people watching him, waiting to see if there was more coming. "It *was* a trap for Josef; a trap that Klaus set up to ensure that his brother lived. Josef had no knowledge of us."

Josef and the men nodded along. It did make sense, but had Klaus done all of this just so he would live? What would have happened if Klaus hadn't been killed by Rissling's cronies on the hill?

Bertrain inhaled deeply and spoke again, "Yes Josef. We would have killed him. You were the traitorous German; he was the "Nazi evil incarnate". He knew he would die. He chose death on his terms, Josef. You weren't the cause. You were the solution."

Chapter 40

Bertrain moved to the other side of the table near Hanna. "You were never fed extra until Eva was gone, because there was no need to. After Eva was lost to Hanna, did you sneak extra rations to her mother?"

Josef shook his head, "No. I just made sure she didn't have to do as much as she normally would. I tried to find other things for her to do."

Bertrain nodded. "Eva…it was Klaus wasn't it? Klaus brought your momma and Marta food. He made sure your momma was healthier."

Eva looked up at Josef and then over to Hanna. "Klaus said only bad kittens talked to much and that I couldn't tell you, else you would stick your big fat nose in and ruin all his plans."

Hanna looked down at her hands. She didn't understand any of this. The foul guard who helped to imprison her had made sure she lived. The emotions Hanna had held in for so long came boiling to the top and she wept. At first it was silently into her hands and then deep soul cleansing sobs. She never heard when everyone assembled but Bertrain, the General, Eva and Josef left the tent.

Hanna felt a hand on her shoulder and reached up to grab it. The strength in the grip surprised her. She hadn't thought much about it, but hadn't expected the General's hand to feel so young, or Bertrain's hand to feel so calloused. She gripped harder and sobbed more. "Here momma. Use this." Eva pushed a worn handkerchief into her hand. Hanna gave the hand on her shoulder another squeeze in thanks and looked up. She left her hand entwined for just a moment as she met Josef's blue eyes, red rimmed with unshed tears in them. He squeezed her hand back and slowly withdrew his hand to turn away to the wall of the tent and wipe his eyes. "Klaus would be rolling his eyes at all this mush" he muttered to himself.

"I'm sorry Josef." Hanna spoke softly, truthfully and then turned back to Eva, her full attention on her hurting child. "Tell me about those sandwiches that Klaus hated."

Eva began chattering away to her mother and Josef looked back one last time. This beautiful girl belonged with her mother, not him, not a soldier like him. He made it to the door of the tent when he changed his mind. He wouldn't walk out on Eva like this. He walked back to the pair and listened as Eva recalled the cake. Klaus had burned it to a crisp and had cursed for days. He had no idea Klaus had fed Hanna and Marta. He also had no idea how they managed to actually eat his late friends cooking.

Josef knelt next to Hanna and met her eyes. "Could I trouble you one last time to talk to Eva?" Hanna nodded and stood to leave. "I have to get my suitcases anyway. Eva and I leave for America this afternoon." Josef nodded and looked at the ground beneath his feet.

After a long pause he stood and then sat in the newly vacated chair and pulled Eva into his lap. "Eva, it's time you and your momma went on your own way now. I was just a step in your path of life. I came to help, and now I have to go. I wrote this down a few days ago. It's my address where I can pick up my mail. You will always be in my thoughts, little kitten, and you can write me a letter anytime you want."

Eva took the small piece of paper. "It's ok Josef. Momma can't keep secrets very good. I knew we were going to leave. She pulled a small folded piece of paper from her dress. "It's a picture of me and you and Kraus walking away from the camp. See the wires of the fence in the dark spot? Right here is the rainbow where Kraus went to" She pointed to the corner of the paper, "And right here at this star is where you will be."

Eva held both her small hands on Josef's face. "You saved me. You saved me like a Papa would. I love you Papa." Her voice broke and she ran out of the tent towards her and Hanna's tent.

Josef heavily leaned back in his chair. He didn't know where he would go, but he would come back often to the home of his parents and check his mail. He too would be leaving this place. He had been exonerated by his help and testimony to the American's on the camp. There were too few American's to be able to liberate Majdanek, but Intel had it known that the Russians were on their way. And they were. They would liberate the camp just a few months later on July 23, 1944. When all was said and done over 360,000 innocent people were murdered in Majdanek.

Hanna sat on her porch, watching the coming sunset and pondered her life and death experience. Eva was 10 now with a brilliant, inquisitive mind. She had always been smart, but where Hanna found herself terrified and stricken with so much anxious energy in new situations, Eva seemed to just take charge. Hanna hated it, but she knew that Josef and Klaus were to blame for that as well. Her child had flourished in an internment camp, while others had withered away to nothing but a wisp of smoke from an always hungry oven chimney.

She thought of the War and her role in it, and wondered only briefly how Josef had fared in their years apart. No matter how she thought of the war and the regime the same question always popped up in her mind.

What could possess an entire population to believe that murder was their own salvation? Surely they too had a God that they would one day answer to? What and how could something go so wrong in such a relatively short amount of time?

The worst and best of humanity flourished during those dark years. Many a good man would shed his life's blood to protect those innocent victims. He would die never knowing their names, but he would die nonetheless. Millions had died. Hanna sniffed, feeling the old familiar pain and remembering.

She had no idea that years later, many an old soldier would lean back in his chair, his eyes glistening as he would remember a horror so long ago, but so fresh as though he were reliving it again.

The Nazi's that were spared the trial, jail sentences and the noose would live on. Perhaps they would live with regret, not sleeping, hearing the cries of those they had pushed to their death. Yet some evil men would sleep well believing in that part of history that they had taken part in, and they would unknowingly...or purposefully keep that same hatred alive.

Some though, would never for the duration of their lives, sleep well again. Haunted for the rest of their lives with the cries of those they had killed.

Chapter 41

Josef spent the last years mostly alone. After his escape from Majdanek, he discovered he was no longer welcome with his old second family. Klaus's family. He missed the brother he had had for so long, and the extra family that had come with him. Over the years he had corresponded with the American, Will, via letters. He poured out his shame that his best friend would go down in American history as nothing more than an evil man.

If Josef wants to clear his friend, he has to be called into the tribunals and also be on trial where many of the same officers who were on trial would just call him on the atrocities that they themselves had done. To let him die for their sins.

To clear Klaus, is to allow himself to be implicated. He lets his own friend go down in history as nothing more than a murderer. Will had helped him through the terrible loss and guilt, and that was where Josef was heading now. He would live out the rest of his days in a small southern town in the American State of Georgia, where he had at least had one true friend. A soldier, a good man.

Will had understood his grief and his loyalty, and had helped him in many ways. Most of which just by being the friendly guy he was. Maybe Josef would look for Eva and Hanna. Eva's last letter was still folded neatly in his wallet. "Josef, I love you. We are moving to another place. Momma found a job as a botanist for a big garden company somewhere in the south of America here. I miss you. I wish you could write me back."

Eva didn't know, but Josef had written back to every single letter she had ever written. He poured his heart out in them. Not to a five-year-old, now a ten-year-old, but to the last link of his old friend. The last living person he could, at least in theory, talk to who had loved his brother as he had.

Hanna watched from her porch as the bus rolled past her house heading down town. The same bus came every day at 6pm. She liked it, it was routine. She never completely overcame her time in Majdanek and unconsciously kept some of the same habits she had incurred while in imprisoned in the hellish death camp. Hanna liked routine, she liked order and for things to be in the right order. She wasn't a big fan of change, and it was tough to handle a bright and spontaneous child like Eva who seemed to thrive on all the change and disorder she could get!

Hanna smiled inwardly as she thought of her beautiful Eva. She was sure a fierce spit fire. She had grown tall and straight and tough, wow that girl of hers was tough. Many times Hanna wished she had a man in her life to help bring a sense of…well a sense of something her daughter was lacking.

She sighed. She had no intention of going out and looking for any man to fill that position. She had all she needed right here in her neat house with its cozy porch and where the whistle sounded every day at noon and the bus rolled by leaving a trail of Georgia dust every day at six.

Josef stretched as he disembarked from the bus. It had been a long three days riding that rough old thing. He was looking forward to finding a place that he would call home, but first he had to find his friend Will. He unfolded the directions and looked around to get his bearings. No time like the present to surprise his buddy and his family. "Must be around supper time anyway. That's never a bad time to surprise someone." He chuckled at his own joke even as his stomach growled. His friend still lived a day's walk away.

A screen door slammed as he walked past a row of neat houses at the edge of town. He sure could live in a small, comfortable town like this. Will lived the next town over where the bus didn't have a route to. With any luck he could catch a ride, or at least find a decent spot to camp along the route.

When the same screen door slammed again Josef stopped on the sidewalk and looked up. A thin young woman sat on her porch sipping something. "She sure slams the door loud for such a tiny thing," he thought as he continued the walk to his future. He walked closer to the neat home with its small porch and stopped suddenly. He heard a bunch of kids talking behind him and moved to the side of the road.

Up ahead another small gang of kids were walking down the opposite side toward him. He glanced at his watch, smiling when he saw it was in fact supper time. All the kids were heading home to eat.

One of the bigger boys broke out of the gang of kids across the street and ran toward the group of kids that just passed him on the sidewalk.

The big kid yelled, "I saw what you did to my brother! I'll do the same thing to you, you little runt."

At the movement in his peripheral vision he saw the young woman from the porch running towards the children. The bigger boy kept stomping and a small kid broke ranks. It was a young girl marching toward the big boy. Head up high, ponytail flying behind her as though not a care in the world.

The woman ran closer and yelled, "No! You kids stop it this instant!"

The bigger boy advanced on the small girl his hands clenched, and Josef stepped up his pace. He didn't want to start a fight with a 12-year-old boy, but he damn sure couldn't let this bully beat up a girl right in front of him!

He came to a dead stop as the young girl spoke, goose pimples spreading up his arms. He knew that old insult like that back of his hand "Oh yeah? I whupped him and I'll whoop you too you damned dummkopf, clumsy assed, dress wearing …"

"…flat footed, good for nothing hundin" Josef finished the curse. The girl turned, met Josef's eyes and ran back to him all but throwing herself into his arms!

"Josef!" She hugged him tightly and he was amazed at how tall she had grown, and so beautiful! He was amazed at the pride he felt in his heart. She was always a pretty thing, all those years ago, but wow… and of all the things she could have gotten from his brother, he sure didn't expect his big old mouth!

Josef smiled and put her down as he watched Hanna walk towards him. She tightened her lips, but her eyes were not unkind. He shook his head in wonder, of all the places he could have been, he ended up right here. He smiled again as he looked down at Eva and pulled a section of her hair like Klaus used to yank on her ponytails.

"Of all the damn places to find myself…"

Hanna met his eyes and struggled to suppress the smile she could feel brewing. She *knew* something would happen to mess up her nice routine. And it came strolling in as this ass right here. She looked down and kicked some dirt on the sidewalk. This was not at all what she wanted to have happen to her tonight...or ever. That ass just waltzed right back into her life.

"You can't come in. I can't have you here. I don't want you here. Anywhere."

"I know. I wasn't asking Hanna. I'm moving to a town just a few more miles up the road. I was invited there. I never knew you were here."

"I wanted it kept that way, Roehm."

They stood looking at each other, while Eva held Josef's hand and then wrapped his waist in another hug. "I missed you Josef. Will you come back and tell me about all your life?"

Hanna shook her head no as Josef looked down into the cute brown eyes looking up at him. His girl. His little girl. Klaus's stray kitten. He could almost feel Klaus beside him as he heard an old memory on the distant whistle of an evening train. *Mein kleines katzchen.*

Josef grinned as he answered Eva, "I'll try honey. I'll sure try."

Made in the USA
Monee, IL
06 June 2023